FREAKSHOW

IN PIECES

A BLACK FALLS HIGH NOVELLA

A DARK BULLY ROMANCE

K.G. REUSS

BOOKS FROM BEYOND

This one's for the boys.

I'm not afraid to die. I'm afraid to live without the threat of death because, really, where's the fun in being safe?

— COLE SCOTT, IN CHAOS

FOREWORD

As always, please note the trigger warnings for this book/series. This book is told from the guys' POV. It takes place between In Silence and In Chaos. This book is a dark bully reverse harem. There are adult situations and multiple love interests.

Suspend disbelief and enjoy the ride because anything is possible at Black Falls High.

We do so love the torment.

CHAPTER 1

COLE

 stared at myself in the mirror, taking in my all-black attire.

Dressed to kill.

Except the killing had already been done.

The baby. *Our baby.* He'd tried to take my family from me.

I blew out a breath and straightened my black, silk tie. I fucking hated funerals. They were a culmination of the end of one miserable life and often lead to the birth of another life to take the place of what had been lost.

In Ian Hall's case not much had been lost. That piece of shit had hurt her. *Had nearly killed her.* Fuck, he'd try to kill what was mine. The life growing inside her had almost been taken by his insanity. That wasn't even the worse part. My Rosebud was unconscious in a hospital bed with a tube helping her breathe. And the baby? Who knew.

Knowing at any moment I could get one of the worst phone calls of my life, within days of the last one, made anger course through my body. All at the hands of a maniac who wanted her so much, he'd have killed to have her.

Like I was one to talk. I'd killed for her too.

Seeing her lying in that hospital bed, unconscious, gutted me.

Knowing she could wake up any day now and hate me for not being there for her tore my soul to shreds. Not that there was much left to it. I'd given a piece of it away the night I ended Ian's life. I'd do it again though. I knew I would.

Sickness had taken over my body and made its home within me. But no one but those closest to me would ever know it was me who killed him. He'd died in the accident. That was what the cops said. His neck had been broken. We'd tried to save them both.

We were heroes.

I snorted at the label the news had given us. I'd never be a fucking hero. In this story, I was the villain.

If Rosalie and my baby weren't enough to kill for, then Ethan only added to it.

Fuck. Ethan. A gunshot to the chest.

My phone rang, pulling me out of the darkness.

"You ready? I'm outside," Fox grunted in my ear.

"I should go to Rosalie. Ian is dead. *She* needs me."

"We need to make an appearance. You heard what Enzo said. We'll go to Rosalie after."

I ground my teeth together. I'd heard Enzo and Fox talking when they thought I couldn't hear them. How they thought I needed a break from shit. How I shouldn't be under too much stress with all the things happening. How I could snap. They'd taken to making decisions for me. If I didn't eat, they'd force me. If I wouldn't talk, they'd sit in silence with me, even when I demanded they leave. And if I needed to fuck shit up, they were at my side, creating chaos with me.

I'd be lying if I said it wasn't a nice break from reality because my head was seriously fucked. Now that I'd let out the monster within me, it was hard to contain it again. There were so many more who deserved to pay. Fox, Ethan, and Enzo always knew I was a ticking time bomb. Hell, I knew it. It was only a matter of time. But when I went off, it had started a chain reaction.

Returning to the man I was would never happen. Something snapped within me that night. Something that could never be repaired.

Fuck. Maybe I'd been broken from the start. The snap was just a fine line between my sanity and insanity breaking its hold on me.

"Whatever. I'll be out in a minute." I hit END on the phone and looked at myself one more time in the mirror.

Mother always said I had eyes made for evil deeds. Maybe that was why she never held me as a child and why she didn't love me. I didn't blame her. After all, who could ever really love the devil?

And now, a killer.

CHAPTER 2

"How was Rosalie this morning?" my father, Anthony, asked as he straightened his tie in the back of the black stretched SUV which was taking us to the funeral.

"Alive," I answered, tearing my gaze away from the bare trees as we passed by in the limo. The leaves had long fallen away, a warning cold was coming. "The machines are still helping her breathe."

He nodded. My mother patted the top of my hand reassuringly but said nothing. Mom liked Rosalie, at least what she'd met of her when I'd brought her home that one time. Father had never had the pleasure.

"I'm impressed with how you've handled everything. And how you cleaned it up," Father continued.

"Learned from the best." I glanced at Emilio who winked at me.

Emilio was Father's righthand man. The guy he trusted with his life. He was a second father to me, teaching me all the ways to take care of business, which included cleaning up a crime scene. Six months ago, I would've laughed at it. Now, I knew all those hours sitting in a car watching my father's men work with Emilio at my side had been worth it.

As much as I tried to deny it, this was my life. I was the son of a mob boss, not just some rich kid from the 'burbs. Playing the part of *just* a rich bitch was tiresome. If anything from this entire shitty situation taught me anything, it was that I needed to handle shit. I'd watched my friends fall apart the past week. Hell, I'd watched them fight for their lives too.

"The world is an ugly place," Emilio said. "Too bad you have to see it, kid."

Father studied me with his dark eyes. "Can you handle it, Lorenzo?"

I locked eyes with him. "I wasn't made for this job, Father. I was *born* for it."

"That's my boy." He patted my knee.

Something warped inside me that night nearly a week ago. Holding Ethan in my lap as we waited for an ambulance kept replaying in my mind.

"Hang on, E," I encouraged, pressing down on his wound, his blood soaking my hands and clothes. "Fox and Cole went to get Rosalie. They're going to get her. She'll be fine."

"He h-hurt her."

"Shh." I swallowed hard at the information. What kind of sick prick hurts a woman like that?

"H-He t-t-tried to t-take the b-baby."

My guts twisted at the thought of my poor Sunshine becoming the victim to such a fucking lunatic. Anger boiled low in my guts as I tried to keep myself focused, but all I wanted to do was turn the knife on Ian and send him to hell.

"H-He t-tried to ra—"

"Don't you dare finish that sentence," I choked out. "Think happy thoughts. Think of Rosalie's smile. The way she always smelled like lavender and a summer breeze. How she kissed you and touched you. The way she loves you."

A smile touched Ethan's lips. My hands shook as I continued pressing on his chest. His skin was so pale and waxy. He looked like a corpse in my lap.

"Yes. Just like that," I murmured. "Do you remember when you saw her for the first time?"

Ethan nodded, the smile still on his pale lips.

"She was the most beautiful girl in the room. Remember when you told us about the first time she talked to you?"

He shook in my arms, the light fading in his eyes.

"Come on, stay with me, E. You need to be here for when she gets back," I said, my voice shaking.

Sirens wailed in the distance.

"She needs you. We all do. You'll break her heart if you leave."

"I-I drew her a p-picture. Make sure s-she gets it?"

"You give it to her your damn self," I grunted, holding him tighter as I fought my tears off.

A banging on the front door signaled the arrival of help.

"In here!" I shouted.

The door burst open, and the police came in before the medics.

Ethan was taken from me immediately as the EMTs began working on him. I stumbled to my feet as law enforcement swarmed in.

"Lorenzo De Luca. What a surprise," one of the officers called out.

I didn't bother saying a word, intent on watching Ethan as they clicked the belts into place over him and carted him off to the back of the ambulance.

I made to follow, but someone called out to me, "De Luca. We have some questions for you."

"Did you hear what I said?" Father's voice brought me back to the moment.

"Sorry," I muttered.

He sighed and repeated himself. "I said, *look the part*. Say nothing. If anyone says anything to you, don't show your feelings about any of it. We're here for looks only. Got it?"

"*Capito*, Father," I said, sitting straight.

Father didn't like to see weakness. No tears. No slouching. No emotion. Only cool, calm restraint.

He nodded as the vehicle pulled up to the church. Benny, our driver, got out and opened the door. Emilio stepped out first, followed by my father. I got out next and buttoned my black suit jacket, slipped my designer aviator glasses in place, and held my hand out for my mother. She took it and stepped out in her black dress.

The cool fall air bit at me, but it wasn't the cold that made me shiver. It was the impending situation. Being stuck at this funeral was the last place I wanted to be. I could easily think of ten other things I'd rather be doing, and they ranged from fucked up to more fucked up. Truth be told, I needed a break from the bullshit and drama. I wanted a simple life, not any of *this*. But this was my life. I had to embrace it or get choked by it. So there I was, arms wide fucking open.

We walked together into the church and took a seat near the middle. I wasn't surprised when Cole slid into the spot next to me.

Father liked Cole. To be fair, he liked all my friends, but he always told me Cole would make a great addition to the family and had encouraged me to recruit him. I never thought it was a good idea until I learned of Ian's fate and the reaction it got from Cole.

He'd wept in my arms for all of a minute before he drew himself up and wiped his eyes. He hadn't cried over the moment since, at least as far as I knew. And I didn't think he'd wept over killing Ian that one time. I was certain he'd wept because he knew what Ian had done to Rosalie.

"Fox will be here soon. He's taking a call outside. Mrs. Bishop called and wanted to talk to him."

I nodded, not saying a word.

"The baby is doing well," Cole continued in a whisper. "Docs say they might let Rosebud off the meds soon, so she'll wake up from the coma they have her in. Hopefully, she'll be able to breathe on her own. Her mom said they were going to do some testing this morning to see if she can handle breathing."

I nodded again, my chest clenching at the possibilities.

She'll make it. She's strong. So strong.

"I want to be there when it happens. I *have* to be."

"You will be," was all I said.

We sat in silence as students from school filled in the empty seats. Ian's mom and brother sat in the front. His father stood off to the side, his eyes raking over the crowd. Despite news coming out about the shit Ian had done, people still came to the funeral. When questioned by law enforcement, we'd made sure to paint a vivid picture of Ian's obsession with Rosalie and how nasty a breakup they had. It wasn't a hard sell considering what he'd done to keep her with him. Attempted murder/suicide screamed our truth for us. Case closed.

I watched with narrowed eyes as the place continued to fill up. I supposed morbid curiosity drove most of them. Everyone wanted to see if the rumors were true. News about the incident spread like wildfire through the school. I'd only heard bits of it through social media rumors and the grapevine, but it was enough. For the most part, it seemed half the people were in shock while the other half thought Ian was a little nuts to start with. I'd read a few online stories of girls telling of their encounters with him.

We'd kept all the dirty details about Juliet and us and our own notebook issues under wraps. We didn't need to get any deeper into shit than we already were. So far, we were heroes. We needed to keep it that way. Being four guys who were hot for Rosalie would set the pearl clutchers in town into a fit of crazy, and there was enough crazy already.

"My parents are in the back," Cole grunted. "Think Daniel will cause a problem?"

"Doesn't matter if he does," I answered. "We'll solve it."

Time passed quickly, and it wasn't long before Fox was sliding in next to us.

"How's Rosalie?" Cole asked, clearly worried something had changed in her condition in the last thirty minutes.

"Still a sleeping beauty," Fox said.

"And Ethan?" Cole pressed.

"Better. Docs said if he continues to improve, they'll try to take him off the ventilator tomorrow morning. His tests went well this morning according to his dad. He called after I talked to Rosie's mom."

"And if shit goes south?" I glanced to Fox.

A muscle feathered along his jaw.

"Then they just try again later. His parents are positive he'll pull through. So are the docs last I knew five minutes ago."

"It's been almost a week," Cole grumbled.

"He needed the rest," I said, hoping they'd at least appreciate some humor.

Fox's lips twitched up. "I'm going to tell him you said that."

"Good. I hope he kicks my ass."

CHAPTER 3

FOX

I had a hard time sitting in church, knowing Ian's body was in the casket and people were weeping for him.

The last thing that piece of shit deserved was tears.

Even after part of the story came out in yesterday's paper, people still came to his big send-off.

I was only there because Enzo's family thought it was a good idea. I'd much rather be beside Rosie at the hospital. Not that she was awake. She had a head injury and punctured lungs, so the docs were keeping her sedated to heal. Not to mention all the other shit wrong with her. Broken bones. A stab wound to the stomach. Cuts and bruises. And the wounds from where Ian tried to force himself on her.

The thought churned my guts. We didn't know exactly what went down since Ethan was out of it when we arrived, but it didn't take a genius to figure it out.

Having almost lost both of them had changed my world in an instant. Nightmares about that night plagued me. As I held her in my arms while she struggled to breathe. As I offered her my breath. As I begged her to stay with me. Reliving every moment in slow motion.

I'd spent almost every waking moment with her or Ethan.

Despite things looking up, we weren't out of the woods yet. Ethan's injuries were extensive. He'd required two transfusions since he'd lost so much damn blood, an emergency surgery that lasted hours, and a ventilator. The doctors couldn't believe he was even alive.

Just a fraction of an inch to the left, and he would've died immediately.

Instead, Ian couldn't finish the job and had missed his heart. Ethan's lungs took a hit but fuck it. He was alive. Ethan hated running and cardio anyway. Maybe this would be an excuse for him to sit it out now.

"Friends and family, I want to start by thanking you all for coming today to celebrate the life of Ian Daniel Hall," the minister started.

It took everything I had not to roll my eyes. My fingers dragged through my hair in frustration.

I watched as Ian's dad took a seat at the end of the front row, his leg bouncing and hands clasped, as he stared at his son's mahogany-colored casket. The lid was closed, thankfully, and a photo of him sat on top.

I despised having hatred in my heart, but it was there. I'd lost someone I loved once too. Maybe this was karma. Although, I did pull Ian from the wreckage. Granted, I didn't bother doing much past that to save his ass. I was too concerned with Rosie.

But I *knew* when Cole walked away what would happen.

I hated that I didn't care. But I just. . . *didn't*. Fuck Ian Hall. He deserved what he got.

Deciding he wasn't worth anymore of my time, I tuned out the rest of the ceremony, opting to think of Rosalie and Ethan. I said a prayer for them. My mind raced all over the place, as it had ever since that awful night. Hell, ever since Rosie had stepped back fully into my life. I wondered what I'd say to Ethan when he woke up. What I'd do if he didn't. The same with Rosie. *Would she hate us? Would she blame me for not protecting her?*

"Relax," Enzo said under his breath as I shifted in my seat.

I had to hand it to De Luca. The guy was always cool under pressure. Even with Ethan, he still had his head in the game, not an ounce of panic slipping from him.

Enzo was the fun, playful guy, but I knew to never underestimate him. He was more than his laughter and smooth talk. Beneath that exterior was the heart of someone quite lethal. I'd seen him handle weapons. The dark look in his eyes the past week warned of his lethality. If I knew him the way I thought I did, he was only getting started.

People shuffled around me as some got to their feet to pass by Ian's casket. I spotted Juliet in the crowd, dressed in black with a couple of her friends beside her.

I glanced at Enzo and Cole who both noticed her.

"She's next if she doesn't stop her shit," Cole growled, blue eyes narrowed in her direction.

"Easy," Enzo said. "We don't have time to worry about that. We said our piece. She said hers. Now, we wait."

"She's playing a dangerous fucking game," Cole continued, eyeing her with distaste.

"She knows," I said softly. "Let her make her move. Her ass is on the line too."

"Can't believe I had to fuck that." Cole shook his head and let out a disgusted sigh.

"Let's go. We need to pay our respects," Enzo urged, giving us a nudge.

"Fuck that. You pay your respects. I already did my part." Cole jerked away and spun on his heel. He marched from the church without a backward glance.

"He needs to control himself," Enzo said, narrowing his eyes at the doors of the church.

"He is what he is, and that's a loose cannon."

"The boy will learn," Emilio grunted, moving ahead of us. "He'll have no choice."

Enzo didn't say anything as he moved to join the line.

I cast a look to Daniel Hall. He locked eyes with me, his lips tilted up in a sneer. *My mother's killer.* Hatred coursed through me. It took everything I had not to approach him and send him off with his worthless son.

The sneer turned into a smirk as he regarded me. Prison and death had turned him even more heartless.

Guess Ian didn't fall far from the prick tree.

CHAPTER 5

COLE

I took a hit from my joint and stared out at the graveyard, noting how peaceful it was.

"Smoking is bad for you," a small voice said from beside me.

I glanced down to see a boy with a mop of dark hair at my side.

"This is weed. Trust me. It helps more than hurts."

The boy eyed me for a moment before speaking again, "You were there when my brother died, right?"

I froze and looked at the kid again. *Fuck.* He was Ian's little brother. Andrew or some shit.

"Yeah, kid. I was."

"Did he suffer?" the kid asked.

"No." I shook my head, not wanting to divulge shit to him. Besides, he was a kid and didn't need to know his brother's dark details. Maybe keeping him a hero would benefit him.

"Too bad," the kid murmured, surprising me.

"What?"

"Ian was mean. He hurt us a lot. He hurt Rosalie. My mom doesn't want me to know what he did, but I saw the paper. I can read. I know what people are saying. I told her to leave and tell on him. I thought she would." He kicked at a pebble with his polished, black shoe.

"Is Rosalie going to die too?"

"No. She's going to make it. She has to."

"I hope she does. I really liked her. She was funny. Sometimes she'd play Xbox with me when Ian would let her. Mom hoped Ian would get better with Rosalie. But he didn't. He got worse."

I nodded, not saying anything.

"I'm glad he's gone." He said it so fiercely it made goosebumps tear across my skin.

What the fuck kind of monster was Ian?

"What about the other guy? The one Ian shot? Is he going to be OK?"

"I hope so," I said softly as Enzo and Fox approached.

The kid peered at them.

"Hey, man, what's up?" Enzo greeted him like they were old pals.

De Luca fascinated me. He was always so put-together. How the fuck he did it was beyond me. Nothing touched the guy. I supposed with a father like his being weak wasn't an option. Anthony wasn't exactly known for his sweet side. The man was ruthless. In the past week, I'd seen shades of Anthony shining through in Enzo, overshadowing the funny, playful side we were used to.

At least I won't be a killer alone. Enzo's time was coming. We all knew it.

Since everything went down, he'd really stepped into mob boss mode. Usually, Fox ran the show, but Fox had been out of it since that night on the highway. So had I. And with Ethan currently struggling to live, the task of leader fell to Enzo. He was doing a good job of it, even though he annoyed the fuck out of me sometimes.

"You're Lorenzo De Luca." The kid's gaze traveled to Fox. "And you're Fox Evans. My dad hurt your mom."

Fox nodded tightly as he stared down at him.

"I'm Andy Hall. I'm really sorry for what my dad and brother did to your family. I was just a kid when my dad hurt your mom. I couldn't do anything about it, or I would have. I don't think anyone should have to go through that stuff."

"No truer words," Enzo murmured, surveying Andy with interest.

"Thank you," Fox answered, his voice soft.

I knew the conversation was killing him. Fox had hated Ian, and it wasn't just because of Rosie. The entire shit with Daniel killing Amy weighed heavily on him. I assumed by default, he hated Andy a little bit too even if it wasn't the kid's fault his dad and brother were pricks.

"No. Thank you for helping me and my mom. I wouldn't have saved him either." And with that, little Andy walked away from us to join his mother who was coming out of the church, her eyes red and Daniel Hall at her side.

"Wow. What a little weirdo," I muttered, taking another hit from my joint.

"I liked him," Enzo said. "Kid has balls. Definitely didn't get it from his dad or brother. Might actually turn out to *not* be a piece of shit when he's older."

"One can only hope." Fox's eyes fixed on the boy and his mom. The mother gave us a slight nod before looking away.

"Whatever." I glanced over to the people walking to the gravesite. "Can we go yet?"

"No. We finish this when Hall is buried. Closure." Enzo fixed me with a stern look.

Knowing he wouldn't let me out of it, I relented. With Enzo's proclamation, we walked to the gravesite, but halfway there, Fox stopped and peered at the church.

"What are you doing?" I followed his gaze.

"I'll be right back."

Before Enzo and I could respond, he loped off toward the church, his head down.

"What the fuck do you think he's doing?" I murmured.

"If I had to guess, I'd say he's going to say goodbye," Enzo answered softly.

"Like he's going to go talk to a dead body?"

"We all have different ways of having closure. This is Fox's," Enzo said easily. "I think you and I need to see him in the ground while Fox just needs to speak."

"When the fuck did you get so wise?" I snorted at him.

A tiny smirk turned his lips up. "I've always been wise, Scott. I was just keeping it hidden until it was needed."

"De Luca, if you had any more secrets, you'd set the world on fire with all your hidden knowledge."

He winked. "Guess you'll have to wait and see."

I let out a soft chuckle. "Whatever you've got hidden, count me in."

"I included you the day I met you, Cole. And the only way out is if I kill you."

This should've made me balk. Instead, it only made me smile. The old Cole was dead. My crazy was free in the world. I may as well make use of it.

"Well, buddy…" I clapped him on the shoulder. "Guess we're in it for the long haul. What do you need done?"

His eyes darkened, and his smirk turned sinister. "Do you still keep the other notebook?"

The Shit List. I nodded.

"I think we're going to need it."

CHAPTER 6

FOX

$\mathscr{I}$ moved past the people filing out of the church and focused on the mahogany casket in the room. I needed to get there and say what I needed to before I lost my shit. I'd only walked past it earlier, not even bothering to cast it a glance.

"Do you need a moment, Son?" the minister asked kindly as I stopped in front of the casket. They'd opened it.

I swallowed hard. "If I could."

The minister gave my shoulder a gentle squeeze and stepped away from me, leaving me with Ian's body. I stared down at him, my heart aching. Not because I was sad the prick was gone. Quite the opposite.

They'd done good with the makeup. The bruises on his face were barely visible now. His dark hair was combed back. I didn't think I'd ever seen the guy's hair combed. It was always a mess. He was in a dark suit and tie. He lay there in such a way that if I hadn't known better, I'd have thought he'd passed away peacefully, rather than from having his neck broken by one of my best friends.

My bottom lip trembled as I stared down at him.

"You son of a bitch," I whispered, my eyes burning. "You didn't have to fucking die. If you'd just let her go. Your blood isn't just on Cole's hands. It's on all of ours. You hurt so many." I stopped talking and wiped at my eyes before continuing, "Your father took my mother, and then you tried to take Rosalie and the baby. I hope your evil died with you. *I fucking pray it did.* All you had to do was let her go. *Why couldn't you just let her go?* Why couldn't you just walk away?"

A sob left my lips as I stared down at him.

"Rosalie and Ethan will relive that night for the rest of their lives if they make it out of this, and the rest of us will live with the knowledge of what you did to them. It didn't fucking have to be this way, Ian. What were you *thinking*? I-I even tried to save you. What the fuck does that say about me?" I wept softly.

"It says you're a good man." Enzo's father rested his hand on my shoulder.

I hadn't heard him approach. He must have seen me come in and decided to follow.

I looked to him and shook my head. "Am I? It's all *my* fault. I'm no better than he is. None of us are good enough for her."

"None of us are good enough for our women. You'll spend your life trying to be, though. And that's what matters."

I wiped at my eyes again. "I don't know what the fuck I'm doing anymore."

"Existing. We all do it after tragedy. Find peace in life, Fox. Not everyone who dies deserves it, but trust me, this one did. Feel your pain, then move on. If you dwell on it, it'll end you too."

I nodded and let out a sigh.

"Enzo is going to take over for me someday."

"I know."

"He could use you at his side. He could use you now. You boys have grown together."

I swallowed thickly. "Enzo is one of my best friends. We share everything."

Anthony gave me a knowing look. "I know you do. That's why I'm telling you to think about your future, Fox. Enzo's life won't be like yours. If you're going to share everything, that means your lives will merge. Make sure it's what you want. Don't live with regrets. Make the choice and deal with the consequences."

"Rosalie?" I whispered, taking in his features. Enzo looked a lot like him. Tall, dark, muscular, eyes of midnight. Enzo was just coming into his power. Anthony oozed it. The man could command a room with a simple look.

He nodded. "Yes. Enzo is in love with her. You all are. He won't let her go so easily. Will you?"

"No," I murmured.

"That's what I'm saying. If you *want* her, you get the package from what I've observed, because my son will fight to keep her, even from you, Fox. You're either *in* or you're *out*, and if you're out, you're alone. Enzo will not follow. He's committed to this life. If he needed any prompting, it happened the night Rosalie and Ethan were harmed."

"I know. I don't want to take Rosie from him. We're *together*." The words were hard to say because I didn't even know if Enzo had told him about our unique situation. In that moment, I realized Anthony De Luca knew a lot more than I thought he did.

"Are you?"

"Yes. I'm in," I said it firmly, my eyes locked on his. I knew being *in* meant more than sticking around. It meant I'd be part of a life I'd never really considered before. Enzo was my friend. Rosalie was our girl. I'd never make her choose. I'd go where she went, and if that was with us all, then I was so fucking in.

"Good. Come. Leave this monster to the worms." He rested his hand on my shoulder and steered me from the church where Emilio met us. He offered me a nod, which I returned. I was grateful for the cool air. I felt like I was suffocating.

"I know you killed my boy," the voice came from my right.

I turned to see Daniel Hall. He dropped the cigarette he'd been smoking onto the ground and snuffed it out with his foot. My body shook. I tightened my hands into fists as I glared at him.

"Just because I killed your mom, didn't give you the right to take him from me," Daniel continued, his eyes hard as he glared at me. "The night your mom died, I went to the car to see if she was OK. *She wasn't.*" He let out a rasping laugh which had me grinding my teeth. "She was babbling and crying. Begging me to help her. To tell her family she loved them. You can't help the dead, though. And now, I'm glad I ran instead of calling for help. She died alone."

"You son of a bitch," I snarled, launching myself forward.

Anthony caught me before I could punch the piece of shit in the face, and Emilio stepped in front, his back to me.

I wasn't sure what he said because he spoke soft and fast to Daniel as Anthony tugged me away, but Daniel's face hardened until he was backing away.

"What the fuck happened?" Enzo demanded, coming over to us with Cole at his side. Enzo's gaze zeroed in on Daniel before moving back to me.

"Nothing." Anthony released me and nodded at me. "You good?"

"Yeah." My voice shook.

"Never let them see your weakness. Keep yourself in check. We don't need to make a scene." Anthony rested his dark gaze on me.

"I know. I'm sorry." I ran my fingers through my hair. "He's just a fucking prick."

"It's OK, man." Cole clapped me on the back. "Let's just get this fucking day over with. We have better shit to do."

"You're right."

I peeked over Emilio's shoulder to find that Daniel had joined Cindy and Andy. She looked like she wanted to run away. Her gaze kept darting around like she was looking for an escape route. Andy stuck close to her side. I had a feeling he might be a good kid and would probably die to protect his mother. I hoped it wouldn't ever come to that, but if he turned out anything like his old man or brother, death couldn't come soon enough.

"I don't think I can do this," I said softly, glancing to Enzo.

He nodded. "Go see Sunshine. Check on Ethan. Cole and I will finish this. We'll be there later."

"Thank you. I'm sorry—"

"Don't apologize. You had your closure." Cole gave me an even look. "I'll ride back with Enzo."

I nodded and hugged each of them before turning my back and marching away. I hadn't made it to my Jeep when I heard Juliet call out to me. Groaning inwardly, I turned and watched her approach me in her black dress and high heels, looking like she was a fucking grieving widow.

"What do you want?" I growled at her. "I thought I made myself clear—"

"Is it true?"

"Is what true?"

"One of you got Rosalie pregnant. You guys were cheating on me with her, knowing full well what I have on you."

"Where did you hear that?" I demanded.

"Read the paper, Fox. It was in this morning's news about how Ian lost his shit and tried to carve the baby out of her. Is it true?"

"Yes, it's true," I snarled. *How the hell had it even gotten out?* I didn't think *that* was a detail the news needed to report.

Her eyes wavered as she stared at me. "Who's baby is it?"

"All of ours, not that it's any of your fucking business, Juliet. We're done here." I spun to get into my Jeep, but she grabbed my arm.

"We're *not* done here, Fox. *Not even fucking close*. I want what's mine. You're my boyfriend—"

I yanked her around and shoved her against my Jeep. She let out a gasp and stared up at me.

"I *do not* belong to you, Juliet. I don't even fucking like you. I did what I did with you *only* to keep Rosalie safe, but that's over now. I won't hurt her anymore. You're out. She's in. And if you continue to fuck with any of us over it, you'll be sorry."

"Because you'll kill me like you did Ian?" she demanded, glaring up at me, her eyes filled with tears.

"I didn't kill Ian. I tried to save him," I snapped back. "He was already dead, which is just as well since he didn't deserve to live after what he did. He was a fucking monster. You're not too far behind."

"I love you, Fox." She reached out for me and brushed her fingers against my cheek.

I flinched away from her.

"I don't want to release everything—"

"Then don't, Juliet. It's that fucking easy. Your ass would burn too."

"But I want what I *want*. If tearing *her* to bits is how I get you free of her, then I'll do it."

"What part of this entire thing don't you understand, Juliet? Huh? *I don't love you.* Never did. None of us do. None of us want you. We want *her*. We'll *never* want you. Every fucking thing you do pushes us further away. You're making it worse. Just. Stop."

A tear slid down her cheek. "You're going to be sorry, Fox."

"I already am, Juliet. You're really pushing me to my limits. Just give me the rest of the videos, and we can call it good."

"I'll give you the rest if you leave her and be with me. Just me and you." She reached out for me again and took my face in her hands. "I'll leave the others alone. I'll leave her alone. You'll have everything."

"You know that won't work, Juliet. What makes you think I'd stay once I had everything?" I asked, glaring down at her.

"Because I know you'll love me back. I'll be better. We'll trust one another. It'll be like it was with us in the beginning. Don't you remember how we were? You used to tell me how much you cared about me. You'd kiss me and touch me and promise me things. Please, Fox. I swear on everything that I'm being honest. Just come back to me and leave her. You'll have it all."

"How would I know you're not lying?"

"Because I want you," she choked out. "I'll give you anything if you come back to me."

I ground my teeth as I stared down at her.

"If the baby's yours, I won't interfere. You can still have that." Her hands shook as she cradled my face. "Please, Fox?"

"I need to think about it," my voice shook as the words came out. There shouldn't be any fucking thing to think about, but I wanted to keep Rosalie safe. I also knew trusting Juliet wouldn't get me anywhere. I needed to hear what Rosalie wanted. She'd decide for me when she woke up. If she didn't want me anymore, I'd walk. I'd slink back to Juliet and continue to protect Rosie. But if Rosie said she wanted me, we'd just have to figure out another way because there wasn't a force in heaven or hell that could make me leave her side if she was in as deep as I was.

"OK," she breathed out. "OK. Take some time. I know you're going through a lot."

I nodded tightly. "I'll be in touch." I jerked away from her before she could try to kiss me or some other bullshit and opened the door to my Jeep.

She stepped away from me and watched me close the door and buckle in. I didn't cast her another look as I sped away.

I didn't need to. It didn't matter if I had to continue to eat shit for a little while longer with her. In the end, she wasn't my future.

Rosalie was.

CHAPTER 7

ENZO

After the burial, we went back to my place and got my car before stopping by a flower shop where Cole grabbed a white rose for Rosalie. He'd been making it a point to bring her a rose every day. Any other time I would've given him shit about being such a softie, but it would be in bad taste now, considering. I figured it was an outlet for him. A way to show his affections for her. We all knew how guilty he felt about leaving when he'd heard about the baby.

When we got to the hospital, we sat in the parking lot for a bit. Cole lit up another joint and passed it to me. I took a hit and leaned back in my seat, giving it back to him. We relaxed quietly, staring out the windshield at the red brick monstrosity that housed the sick and dying. I both loved and loathed the place. For one, it saved my girl's life and the life of one of my best friends. But I hated it too because it couldn't make things go faster to bring them back to us.

"Fox almost lost his shit today," Cole commented, blowing out smoke and coughing.

"I expected that. He's been in love with Rosalie since they were kids. Knowing Ian tried to kill her plus all that other shit with the Hall family… and it was a disaster waiting to happen."

We both grew somber again and each took another hit.

"You wonder what we'll do if Rosalie wakes up and tells us to fuck off?" Cole asked.

"No, because I already know what I'll do."

"What's that?"

"Carry her sexy ass over my shoulder to my bedroom and keep her there forever."

Cole chuckled before he was silent for a moment. "I'm worried she won't want me. I bailed on her when she needed me. I wouldn't blame her. I'm a real piece of shit for doing that to her and the baby."

I slid my gaze over to him. He stared down at his lap, his hands trembling as the small gift on his lap bounced from his twitchy movements. Today, he brought a gift with him for Rosalie in addition to the rose. I had no idea what he'd wrapped in that box, but I knew it had to be something special. Cole wasn't the gift giving sort.

Fox and I hadn't spent a lot of time discussing the matter of Rosalie with him. It was a touchy subject we figured he needed to address first. Anything we said would just sound like we were placating the crazy bastard.

"I've never been in love before. I don't know what the fuck I'm doing. It's terrifying me."

I nodded. "Same, but I know she wants us. I'm not worried. If she doesn't, we'll fight for her. It's that simple."

"Yeah. I'm going to be a dad," he whispered. "*Me.* A fucking father."

I smiled at him as his gaze met mine. "You'll do great, man."

"Will I? I'm a fucking mess. I didn't even know I was capable of loving anyone other than myself until I met Rosalie. What if I fuck all this up?"

"Then you fuck it up and then do better. It's really all any of us can do."

"Again with your wisdom." He shook his head. "Do you think she still wants me?" His voice became soft, his usual confident demeanor falling away to reveal the vulnerability he felt.

I hated to see him so worried and down on himself. This wasn't Cole. He was dark and strong all the damn time. *Intense.* But this guy next to me? This guy was cracking and needed his girl back. Fuck, we all did. Each of has had chinks in our armor since all this shit went down.

"Without a doubt. Just know she's been through hell. Don't push it. I've already told myself she might need some time. If she does, we'll give it to her. We'll give her whatever she needs."

"Would I sound like a total chicken shit if I said I'm scared to see her once she's awake?"

"Yep." I took another hit and blew out the smoke. "But I still love you. And she does too. You'll see."

Cole laughed softly and loosened his tie. "I fucking hate wearing a tie. Feels like a noose."

"Noose. Tie. It's all the same in my fucking world," I grunted, staring out the window and taking another hit.

The memory of seeing Emilio and Jenson, another of my father's men, choke a man to death with his own tie flashed through my mind. It was a blue tie with fucking yellow ducks on it. At the time, I'd thought it was absurd until I read in the paper the guy had a kid. The tie was probably a gift from his kid. I'd helped carry the body after it was over. Nothing like a little bonding time with the family and an ugly fucking memory to keep a guy warm at night.

"Let's do this." Cole got out of the car and ran his fingers through his hair.

I followed a moment later.

"I'm going to go see Ethan. I'll give you some time alone with Rosalie," I said as we stepped into the hospital lobby.

Cole nodded, the rose and gift in his hand, and got into the elevator beside me.

"You going to talk to Fox?" Cole asked as the elevator rose.

"Yeah. I'm sure he's trying to figure out his next move, but he fucked us last time. It has me concerned. He loves Rosalie so much, I'm worried about what he'll do to keep her safe, especially after all this shit happened."

"That's the problem, isn't it? He's willing to do anything to protect her." Cole let out a sigh. "We all are."

I nodded. "I'll talk to him. Make sure we're all on the same page.

We take down who we need to from the other notebook. Nothing more. You know the plan."

Cole nodded tightly, a muscle popping along his jaw.

The elevator dinged, and we got off. Cole went right while I went left. The good thing was, Ethan and Rosalie were on the same floor, just at opposite ends.

"Hi," a young nurse addressed me, her cheeks reddening as she took me in. "A-Are you family?"

"I am. I'm his brother," I answered, looking her up and down and giving her a smile. Just because I was in love didn't mean I'd forgotten how to bend a woman to get what I wanted. It was all innocent. I didn't want the twenty-something nurse. "What's your name?"

"Betsy," she answered breathlessly. "Uh, you can go in. He's still out."

"Do we have any news on what's going on? Any changes?"

"His vitals look good. The doctor wants to try to get him off the ventilator to see how he's doing. When we did a test run with him earlier, it seemed promising."

I nodded at her. "Should I be concerned?"

"There's always a reason for concern. But I think after what he's been through, he's proven he's a fighter. We have good medicine on our side too. I have faith in his fight and our ability to handle anything that may come up."

I gave her another smile. "So do I." I swiveled and went into his room, my heart clenching.

Ethan's pale body lay on the bed, that damn machine helping him breathe. He looked like he was wired for sound. He'd lost some weight, his bulk having shrunk quite a lot in the past week. Ethan was a powerhouse. Muscles. Stamina. The past few months had taken a toll on him though. It started when Rosalie walked out on us. Now this shit happened.

I took a seat at his bedside and rested my hand over his cool one. White bandages wound their way around his wrists where he'd been cut.

My jaw hurt from clenching my teeth. Knowing what Ethan and

Rosalie had been through ate at me. Had I been on the road that night with Fox and Cole, Ian wouldn't have died. Not right then, anyway. I'd have taken him back to one of our warehouses and fucked with him until he was begging for his life. Then I would've cut his throat and watched him bleed out, choking on the last bit of life left in him. Cole was far too kind by ending him in such a quick way.

"Hey, E," I greeted Ethan softly. "It's Enzo. Cole and Fox are with Rosalie down the hall. She's doing better. The baby is still hanging on. They're going to let Rosalie wake up soon. The doctors said you did good on your tests today, so maybe we'll be talking tomorrow. I hope so, man."

My breath caught in my chest as Ethan's finger twitched beneath my hand. A first since he'd been out.

"Can you hear me?" I murmured, searching his face for any signs of him hearing me. *Nothing.* I cleared my throat and spoke again, "Everyone at school has been asking about you. You're famous. I stopped in there earlier this week to pick up some assignments. You know how my mom is about education. My dad, well, you know what he thinks is important."

Ethan's finger quivered again. Excitement coursed through me, so I continued, "I hope you wake up tomorrow, man. We've missed you, E. I was so scared we were going to lose you. I prayed." I let out a soft laugh. "You know me. I never pray."

Another spasm, this time it was two fingers.

"Man, I can't wait until you're awake. Both you and Sunshine. Then we'll all be together. We'll put all this shit behind us. Cole and I have been talking about buying a place next to the college so we can all live together. Maybe Rosalie will get into Mayfair with us. She's a helluva singer." I paused, my voice cracking. "I miss her voice."

Once again, Ethan's fingers twitched beneath mine.

"We can help raise the baby. Cole is freaking out about becoming a dad. He's afraid he won't be good enough, but I know he will be. He's a good guy." I let out a soft laugh and wiped at my damp eyes. "Can you imagine Cole changing a diaper? I don't think he's thought that far ahead, but man, I can't wait for that. It'll be hilarious."

I grew quiet, watching Ethan in his slumber. A soft knock on the door had me turning my head to see Fox poke his head in.

"Hey. How is he tonight?" He stepped into the room and closed the door behind him.

"Good. I think he can hear me. His fingers move when I talk to him."

Fox approached the bed and settled in the chair on Ethan's other side and rested his hand over Ethan's.

"Hey, man. It's Fox. I brought you a photo of Rosie. It's on the stand beside your bed. It's the one of her in that purple sundress you loved so much. You remember? You snapped it the day before she talked to you. Her smile is so big and beautiful in it." Fox's eyes lit up as he stared at me. "He did it. He moved."

"E, can you hear us? Move your fingers twice for yes."

We both held our breath while we awaited his reaction. A moment later, his fingers twitched twice beneath mine. I grinned at Fox.

"He can hear us."

"Your mom left some clothes here for you yesterday. She and your dad come visit you every day. They're always the first ones here and the last to leave. I have to force them to go home sometimes. They had to go today because your sister had her recital." Fox studied Ethan's face, and a small smile touched his lips. Ethan must have moved for him. "I miss you so much, Ethan. I thought we were going to lose you." Fox's voice cracked. "Waiting for you and Rosie to wake up is torture, and I know you need to heal. But man, I wish you guys would do it faster so I can look you in the eyes when I say I fucking love you. You're my brother. My best friend. You're part of our fucked-up world, and we need you back. So hurry back to us, OK? I already begged Rosie twice today. I'm not above doing it to you too." Fox leaned down and pressed a kiss to Ethan's hand and let out a sigh.

I remained quiet for a moment before I broke the silence. "How was Cole doing with Sunshine?"

"He's a nervous wreck." Fox sighed and recounted what I already knew about Cole's worries regarding Rosalie wanting him still. "But she loves him. I *know* she does. We just need to get past this shitty spot, and then everything will work itself out."

I nodded. "I suppose. I mean, we do still have the Juliet issue to deal with. I really don't think she's grasped the concept of fucking dying. How many times do you need to threaten bodily harm to someone before you have to follow through just to prove a point?"

Fox's Adam's apple bobbed in his throat for a moment before he spoke. "She wants me to come back. You guys will be free if I stay. She'll keep shit hidden."

I cocked my head at him, nausea churning in the pit of my stomach. "Would you be happy?"

He looked at me like I was nuts. "No."

"Then why bother?"

"Because I want to protect you guys. I want to protect Rosalie's reputation. I want to protect everything that *is* her. If she loses everything—"

"Fox, man, I'm going to be the voice of reason here. We don't need protecting, and Rosalie *has* lost everything. Her dad is a fucking sack of shit. I mean, yeah, he's here for her now, but if he'd let her stay home, none of this would've probably happened. So that relationship is already ruined. Rumors are already flying around school about what happened. Yeah, she still has her scholarship, but who fucking cares? She wants to be at Mayfair with us. Cole and I already discussed it. We'll pay her tuition if she needs the help. It's not even a problem. So, tell me, what has she really got to lose now?"

Fox nodded thoughtfully. "You're right. I'm in the same mindset as Cole, I think. What if she wakes up and doesn't want us?"

I laughed softly and looked over at Ethan. "Then Ethan is a lucky man because he gets the girl all to himself."

His fingers jolted again.

I grinned. "Just kidding, E. I'll fight for her."

If I didn't know any better, I'd think the corner of Ethan's lips tried to lift up into a smile.

CHAPTER 8

COLE

fter Fox left me, I sat staring at Rosalie. She looked so tiny in that hospital bed. Her face was a mess of ugly purple and black bruises. Even if she were awake, I didn't think she'd be able to open her eyes since they were still so swollen.

I leaned over and grabbed the brush her mom had left on her bedside table and gently tried to fix her hair, at least the hair I could get to. It fell just past her slender shoulders now. I smiled as a soft tendril curled around my finger. I ran it between my index finger and thumb, my gaze locked on her.

"You're beautiful, Rosebud," I murmured, brushing my knuckles against her jaw. "I wish you'd wake up and smile for me. I miss you so fucking much."

I swallowed and rested my hand on hers.

"I got you a gift. Well, it's for the baby and you." With my other hand, I laid the box on the edge of the bed and popped the lid off. Inside was a yellow onesie with a tiny bear on the chest and a pair of matching socks.

"It's something called a onesie and the tiniest socks I've ever seen. I had no idea what I was doing," I admitted softly. "But I liked this. I thought you would too. Maybe the baby can wear it home from the hospital after she's born." I let out a soft laugh. "I keep thinking the baby is a girl. I'd have a queen and a little princess." I paused for a moment, trying to get my shit together so I wasn't blubbering like a little bitch. "I-I was thinking about names for the baby. I like Violet or Lily for a girl. Then I could have my own flower garden." I laughed softly at how absurd my idea was. *Roses and Lilies.*

"If it's a boy, maybe we could name him after Ethan. I always liked that name, and he deserves the honor since he nearly died trying to save you. It would make for a strong middle name." I paused and let out a breath. "I can't believe I'm going to be a dad. I'm so scared, Rosalie. What if I'm a terrible father? I don't exactly have anything to model it after. My old man has always been too busy for me. I-I don't want to disappoint you more." My voice cracked.

Fuck.

I drew in another deep breath to compose myself. This time, I shifted so I could be closer, my head near her abdomen, and spoke, "*Little blossom,* it's me. Y-your dad. I'm here. I love you so much. I promise when you're born, I'll do my best to keep you safe. Mommy too. I'll teach you how to ride a bike. I'll build you a treehouse. We can spend all of December searching for the perfect gift for Mommy because when she smiles, it's the most beautiful thing in the world. We'll jump in mud puddles together. I'll make you blanket forts and teach you so many things," my voice shook. "I can't wait to meet you."

I rested my head against Rosalie's hand and sniffled. I'd been trying to keep my shit together, but I had a lot on my mind. My tears dampened her skin.

"Wake up, Rosebud. *Please.* I need you." I sat up and rubbed my eyes. I had to get my shit together. At this point, I was weaker than everyone, wallowing in my own shit. Guilt was a bitch. I never should've left her.

"I'm so sorry. I'd go back in time and fix it all if I could. Believe me. Nothing will *ever* harm you again. We have a plan. It's a good one, baby." I let out a sigh as I stared at her. So much anger coursed through my body. So much regret over walking out on her when she told me she was pregnant. If she ever forgave me, it would be a miracle.

Someone cleared their throat from behind me, and I looked over to see the guys. I hadn't heard them come in.

"Sorry," I muttered, wiping quickly at my eyes. I was sure they hadn't seen the tears. I wasn't a crier, but these past few weeks had taken their toll on me.

"Man, don't apologize," Fox said, moving to my side and looking down at Rosalie. He rested his hand on my shoulder. "We've all done a fair bit of begging."

I nodded, my throat tight as I put the lid back on the onesie box and placed it on her bedside table next to the rose. "How's Ethan?"

"He's good. He twitches his fingers when we talk to him." Enzo moved deeper into the room until he was on Rosalie's other side. He leaned down and pressed a gentle kiss to her forehead.

"Good. I owe him so much." I sat back and rubbed my eyes. "I should probably buy him a fucking fruit basket. You guys know how he loves fruit."

The guys chuckled.

"I was thinking we could plan a weekend away once everyone is back on their feet," Fox said, clearing his throat. "A getaway where we can just relax. Some place with a view and a hot tub."

"I'm down with that. I need to get away from this shit hole," I grunted, hating I'd go home later and lie in bed, hearing Ian's ugly words on repeat in my head. Then I'd feel the crack of his neck reverberating through my body. The hatred would boil inside of me. The pain over walking out on Rosalie would finish off what was left of me.

Fox and Enzo both pulled up chairs and sat down.

"Have the Bishops said anything about where Rosalie will go once the hospital releases her?" I asked, glancing at Fox, who had the inside track on that shit show.

He blew out a breath and settled back in his seat, his blue eyes locked on Rosalie. "I don't know. It seems like they want her home. Guess her nearly dying changed her dad's mind."

I ground my teeth and shook my head. My anger was so close to the surface nowadays it took all I had to control myself. My legs bounced. I ran my hands along my thighs and hauled in an even breath.

Fuck her dad. He and I would have our moment.

"Ethan's place would be the next choice, but considering what happened there, I can't imagine that being good for either of them." Enzo sat forward, his dark eyes sliding from Fox to me. "So, I'm thinking my place."

"Your place?" I raised a brow at him, intrigued at his idea. My plan was simply to kidnap her on her release and drive anywhere she wanted to go. No place would be too far.

"Yeah. We have the guest house. It has two bedrooms, not that they'd need it. It's safe there. Shit can't happen with all the security my father has in place, plus the community is gated. And," Enzo rushed on, glancing between me and Fox again, "we can be there with them. Or at least I'll be able to."

Fox snorted and shook his head. "I'm not letting her out of my sight. Wherever she goes, I go."

"Same," I said, nodding.

"Fine. I'll order a big fucking bed. Alaskan king sound big enough for you assholes?" Enzo lifted a dark brow at us, a tiny smirk playing at the corner of his lips.

"I don't know if your fucking ego can fit into it. Better get two," I quipped back, knowing it would get a rise out of him.

His smirk turned into a wide grin, his dark eyes dancing with mirth. "It's the size of my cock we should be worried about. Not my ego."

Fox chuckled as I shook my head.

"You think it's all good now but wait until you wake up spooning me." I waggled my brows at Enzo who snorted.

"Whatever, you fucking jackass. Don't act like you wouldn't snuggle into my arms."

"You're both getting weird." Fox looked between us.

"What's wrong, Foxy? You want to get spooned?" I turned my attention to him.

"Let's get one thing straight. *I* do the spooning, and it won't be with either of you pricks. It's Rosalie I want. You two weirdos can do whatever it is you do when the rest of us aren't around."

Enzo let out a loud laugh. "Cole fucking wishes."

I shrugged, enjoying the banter. It felt good to laugh again.

Enzo smirked and shook his head at me before he spoke. "All joking aside, are you guys down for this? I'll set it up if you are."

I glanced at Fox whose attention was on Rosalie. "I already said my piece. I go where she goes if she'll still have me."

"Same," I murmured, reaching out and gently resting my hand on her abdomen. "But we need to find out what she wants. We saw her answer in the notebook, but that doesn't mean much after what's happened. I'm sure if her old man is back in this shit, he's going to want a say too."

"Rosalie is an adult. She can decide what she wants. And if she can't, I'll decide for her *and* her old man," Enzo said darkly.

"He's a prick," I growled.

I'd only seen him at the hospital. He never tried speaking to any of us except Fox, but I'd seen the way he'd looked at me and Enzo, disgust on his face. I bet he thought about all the dirty things we'd done to defile his daughter. The moment I could say something to him, I would.

I hoped his thoughts drove him fucking nuts at night. He'd earned my hatred the moment Rosalie cried for help. There wasn't much in the world that would ever change those feelings.

CHAPTER 9

FOX

"How was everything?" Dad asked as I stepped into the living room and tossed my jacket on the coat rack.

"Better. At least I'm hoping it is. Ethan's breathing is better. The doctors ran some tests today to see how he'd do with breathing on his own. It went well, so they're going to try to take him off the machines tomorrow morning. I want to be there for it."

I followed Dad into the kitchen and watched as he grabbed two plates from the cabinet. He looked tired. He spent a lot of time working. It got worse after Mom died. I figured it was his way of dealing with shit. Plus being home reminded him too much of what we'd lost. He was a good father, but I missed him.

"I ordered pizza. It needs to be reheated." He dug around in the fridge before pulling out a large pie with the works.

I set the oven for him and we each got a soda.

"How's Rosalie?"

"She's... fucked up," I muttered, sighing heavily. "She's the one I'm really worried about. They're going to see if she can make it through the breathing test tomorrow. If she does well, they'll see about getting her off the machines. Her friend Jamie texted me earlier to tell me she was sure Rosie tried to open her eyes when she stopped by at lunch. I haven't seen anything like that though."

Dad nodded. "I'm sorry, Son. She's a good girl. She's strong. She'll make it through. She's made it this far."

I swallowed hard. "I'm scared."

"I know," he murmured. "I can't make that feeling go away. I wish I could. I wish I could take it all away."

"I know."

"How was the funeral?" He didn't meet my gaze, busying himself with his soda.

"I hated every moment of it. It was nice to know the bastard was buried though." I paused before continuing, "Daniel Hall got in my face. H-He said some nasty shit about Mom."

Dad's piercing blue eyes met mine. "What did he say?"

I shook my head, not wanting to divulge the information. I'd already said more than I should have. "Just that he doesn't regret it."

Dad's hands shook. "He will. Someday, he will."

"I hope so, but even if he doesn't, he'll live knowing he lost out too."

Dad studied me for a moment. "That kid didn't die in that accident, Fox. I'm not stupid."

I stared back at him wordlessly.

"For what it's worth, I'd have done the same." He took a sip of his drink.

"I didn't want it to come to that. I really didn't. I really hoped he'd make the right choices. I-I hoped he'd changed."

"You're like your mom. Always kind and compassionate. Times changed us all, but deep down inside, you're the same sweet kid you've always been. Don't you dare regret taking out the trash, Fox. He hurt Rosalie. He hurt Ethan. He hurt so many more. The kid was going down a path that led him to that moment out there on the highway. That's not on you. Don't ever think it is."

I nodded, my throat tight.

When Dad's arms opened, I stepped into them and let him hug me. It had been so long since he had. It felt good.

"I'm proud of you, Fox. Your mom would be too," he said thickly as he pulled away.

"I hope so."

"She is. I know she is." He smiled sadly. "I miss her."

"Me too," I whispered. I pulled out a stool and took a seat.

"Rosalie is a lot like your mother. Strong. Beautiful. Fierce. You made a good choice with her. I'm glad you found your way back to each other. Your mom always thought you'd run off and marry her. She loved Rosalie so much."

I smiled. "Honestly, Dad, I think I'm going to. I'm so in love with her."

He grinned back at me. "I bet she'll say yes."

I hesitated for a moment, watching as Dad turned and pulled the pizza out of the oven. I hadn't told him about our unique relationship. Honestly, I had no idea how he'd take it.

"Dad?" I cleared my throat.

He slid two pieces of pizza onto my plate and dished out his own.

"Yeah?" He settled at the stool beside me.

I turned and looked him. "I have to tell you something."

The slice of pizza that had been halfway to his mouth was placed back on his plate. "OK."

"You're probably not going to understand it—"

"Just tell me."

I blew out a breath. "I-I'm in a relationship with more than Rosalie."

He lifted his eyebrows at me, confusion marring his face. He pushed his dark hair away from his face, the fine lines around his blue eyes crinkling as he considered what he was going to say to me.

"Don't cheat, Fox—"

"I'm not. It's not like that. Uh, shit," I muttered, taking a moment to gather my thoughts. "Fuck. Dad, I-I'm in a relationship with, uh, Cole, Enzo, and Ethan too."

His eyebrows shot higher on his forehead as he gaped at me. "Uh. . . what? Y-You're gay? Bi-sexual? Fox, I—"

"Let me explain." I licked my lips. "We're *all* in love with Rosalie. We all want to be with her. So we're going to be. W-we have been."

"So Rosalie and you four?" He frowned. "And you're all OK with it?"

I nodded.

"You're all just... together?"

I nodded again.

He shook his head and leaned against his elbows on the table after pushing his food away. I watched, wondering if he would kick my ass out for being too fucking messed up.

"Are you... bi-sexual?"

"No. I'm not attracted to guys. But these guys... they're different. They're my best friends. *I love them.* I don't want us ever to be apart. It's not like we're all *with* one another. We're with Rosalie. But we're all with each other. If that makes sense."

Dad blew out a breath and slid his plate back. "Well, Son, if you're happy, then I'm happy. I say if you're lucky enough to find love, then hold onto it. Even if it is a harem or whatever you kids call this sort of thing. All I know is I love you, and your happiness means more to me than anything."

"Really?" I hadn't expected that response from him. I stared at him wide-eyed.

He grinned at me and took a bite of his pizza. "Really. I don't need more details than that. Now eat. Your pizza's getting cold."

I grabbed my slice, smiling. At least telling him was out of the way. Not being able to talk to him and let him know what was going on had been killing me inside. I wanted him to accept it. Now that he had, it was just one more thing I didn't have to worry about.

"I really am proud of the man you're becoming," Dad repeated softly, biting into his pizza again. "Mom is too. I know it."

"Thanks, Dad." I smiled and chewed my dinner.

He didn't seem the least bit fazed by the news now. In fact, talk swung to inviting everyone over for a bar-b-que once Rosie and Ethan were back on their feet.

I didn't have the heart to tell him about moving out to be with

Rosalie. Easing him in seemed kinder, considering the bomb I'd just dropped on him. Instead, I just wanted to enjoy the evening with him.

"Want to watch the game? I used the DVR." He put another slice of pizza on his plate and grabbed his soda.

"Hell, yeah." I followed him into the living room and took a seat on the couch as he sank into his recliner and turned on the game.

Once Rosie and Ethan were back, life might not be so damn bad. I just had to figure out the whole Juliet thing.

My heart sank as I stared at the screen.

As much as I hated to admit it, I might just have to let Enzo and Cole handle things.

CHAPTER 10

ENZO

"Come." Dad stepped into his office.

Emilio and I followed him inside and took seats in front of his desk. Dad went to the small bar, grabbed three glasses, and returned, pouring us each a drink.

"What's going on?" I asked, lifting the glass to my lips and taking a deep sip. Butterflies soared to life in my chest. Drinking in my father's office meant he had something big to tell me. And by something big, it meant I'd be doing some elbow work.

"In light of the information you've provided me, Lorenzo, I think I may have a gift for you." Father took his seat behind the desk and sipped his scotch before continuing. "You have some petty blackmail bullshit going on, and I didn't want to involve myself in it. However, something of a miracle has fallen into my lap."

"Really?" I placed my empty glass on his desk.

He sat forward and refilled it before looking to Emilio. "Tell him, Emilio."

I picked up my now full glass and looked to my father's righthand man. Tall, dark, lethal. That was Emilio. He smiled at me.

"Melvin Croft. That name mean anything to you?"

"Juliet's father," I answered, shifting in my seat. *Where the hell were they going with this?*

"Correct. It seems he's been playing a dangerous game as well. You know, the kind where there are no survivors?" He lifted a dark brow at me as he tipped his own glass against his lips and drank.

"I'm listening."

Father leaned forward, lacing his fingers together on the desk. "He owes me a great deal of money. He's been getting loans to cover his gambling expenses. He's bankrupted his family." Father leveled his gaze on me. "I don't like when I'm owed things, Lorenzo."

"What do you need me to do?"

"Your father discussed it with me, and I've agreed," Emilio said with a shrug. "It's completely in your hands right now. Whatever decision you make, we'll follow."

"You're testing me." It wasn't a question. I knew what it was. "Again, what do you *need* me to do?"

"We need him to pay. How do we get blood from a rock?" Father surveyed me.

"From the child with the pet rock," I said gruffly.

"Exactly. We're allowing him to live by your will alone. I feel like you might have a better idea, given the current circumstances." Father gave me a Cheshire grin.

I nodded. "You want me to take down his daughter."

"We want *you* to decide what you want to do. We'll give you plenty of time to think it over. Melvin isn't going anywhere. We're giving him what he needs right now and will continue to do so until you've decided his fate. Make sure whatever you decide—his death or... others—is a choice you can live with. Once you command it, it cannot be undone." Father's dark eyes flashed, letting me know he meant absolute business and anything I did would be final.

"I understand."

"Can you handle this. . . *gift?*" Father cocked his head at me.

"I can, Father."

"Good." He opened his desk drawer and pulled out a wrapped box and pushed it toward me.

"What's this?" I glanced between him and Emilio, who simply studied me.

"Open it," Father said.

I tore off the red and black paper and then opened the box.

A new Glock, complete with silencer and a box of bullets.

I swallowed and peered at my father.

"I want Cole, Fox, and Ethan included in this. I don't care how you utilize your men, I only want to know that it was done. Emilio will oversee things. Take your time. I want to make sure you cover your bases, so I don't have to."

Carefully, I lifted the gun from the box and gazed down at the cool, dark metal.

Destiny stared back at me in all her deadly glory. I would be God, deciding who lived and who died.

"Thank you for the gift." I chambered a bullet and smiled. This was exactly what I needed. "No one fucks with a De Luca."

"I'll drink to that." Emilio tipped his tumbler back and finished off his scotch.

I placed the gun back in its box and polished off my drink. The warmth of the alcohol flooded my body. "We'll go shooting soon. I know you're damn good, Lorenzo, but being the best is important. Being clean is important."

"I know, Father. I'm ready."

He smiled at me, the darkness reaching his eyes. "My son, you were born ready."

"Are we killing her tonight?" Cole asked as he held the new gun in his hands. He turned it over and then looked at me as we sat in my car outside his house.

"No. I'm not the sort of guy who runs around offing people. I want to wait to see what she does."

"You're kidding, right? You know what she'll do. She'll go right back to her same old shit, Enzo. Let's just do it. We'll take out her old man too as a little something extra for your dad."

"That's not how this works." I took the gun from him and stowed it in the center console. "We kill what matters most to him, so he suffers. We both know that's Juliet. Next would be Ella, his wife. But since Juliet is causing us some issues, it would seem she'd be the best target for our purposes. However, I'm judge and jury here and will have to live with the decision. I want to make sure I can."

"It's not so bad. Killing someone," Cole said softly. "Especially if you're doing it for someone you love."

I reached out and gripped his hand. "If this happens—"

"I'll do it, Enzo. You don't even need to ask. The blood and burden can be mine."

I surveyed him in the dim light. His usually bright blue eyes bore ugly dark circles beneath them. His blond hair looked like he'd been tugging on it in his frustration and anger. He was exhausted.

Gripping his shoulder, I leaned forward and rested my forehead against his.

"I'll give you time to make the decision. I don't need your answer tonight. Just think about it. OK?" I released his him and closed my eyes, my forehead still against his.

"Deal," he said softly.

I tapped his cheek gently and moved back to my spot, staring out at the night.

"Are you going to ask Fox?"

"I don't know… Fox *needs* to be with Rosalie. I almost think I should let him and Ethan take her away from us. We're dangerous, Cole. Our lives are about to get labeled with a big fucking bright red check mark for fucked up. Do we really want to bring the people we love into that? My world is dark and dangerous. That means their world would be too."

"Do you really want to let them go?" His voice shook.

"I want to save them," I answered simply, resting my head back and peering over at him.

He nodded. "I do too. I'd rather let my garden go than have it endangered."

I knew he was talking about Rosalie and the baby. Fox and I had overheard him telling her about his idea for baby names and how Rosalie and the baby were his little garden. My heart went out to him.

"But I want what I want, Enzo." He pleaded with his big, blue eyes. "I want Rosalie tucked beneath me, her lips around your cock as I make love to her. I want her to stroke Fox and love Ethan. I want it all, man."

I smirked at him. "It's been a long time since her lips were around my cock."

"*Lucky bastard.* I never had the pleasure."

"She's incredible."

"Then let's not let this go. Let them decide what they want. If we're all in, the four of us can protect her and the baby."

I licked my lips. "Maybe we don't have to tell her right now. We can take care of the notebook shit. We'll let her get better before we push this shit on her. And we'll let Ethan heal. God knows he's going to probably have to go back to rehab after all the pain meds that have been pushed through his body."

Cole breathed out. "I like that idea. You and me... We'll handle everything. We'll clear out the second notebook if shit gets bad."

"Together?" I held my hand out to him.

He placed his in mine, his hold fierce.

"Always, brother."

CHAPTER 11

COLE

Today was the day. My boy Ethan would hopefully be coming off the ventilator and opening his damn eyes. Nerves had my guts in a vice, the prospect of things taking a turn for the worse making me sick with worry.

Today was also the day they planned to test Rosalie to see if she might be able to come off her machines.

"Take a hit." I handed the joint over the front seat of Enzo's Mercedes to Fox.

He took it and inhaled deeply. He looked like I did. Dark-rimmed blue eyes, hair a damn mess. The only difference between us was that I'd put on clothes without wrinkles in them.

But Fox? His torn jeans mimicked what Enzo wore, minus the designer label, and his black t-shirt wasn't as snug as it usually was, making me think he'd just snatched it off his bedroom floor and decided to re-wear it for probably the third time this week. He had his leather jacket in place along with his dark beanie. His wrists were adorned with the leather bracelets he always wore.

I watched as he took a second drag before handing it back to me. I passed it to Enzo after my turn and watched as the Italian mob prince inhaled deeply. Enzo had his shit together. Unruffled.

Unwavering. He was a force in his V-neck, white t-shirt. Black canvas moto jacket in place. Rings on his fingers. Leather bracelets on his wrists. His black hair was styled as perfectly as always.

"You're a beautiful man, De Luca," I said, watching as he blew out a puff of smoke.

He grinned at me. "Right back at you, Scott."

"Speaking of being all girly and in touch with our feelings and shit," Fox called out. "I told my dad about us and Rosalie."

"Really? How'd that go?"

"Good." Fox leaned forward and rested his arms on the tops of the front seat. "Great, actually. I thought he'd lose his shit. He actually seemed happy for me. For us."

"Nice," Enzo commented, taking another hit.

"So if I grab your ass in front of him, he won't kick mine?"

Fox snorted. "Doubt it, but I'd really rather you keep the ass play to the bedroom."

"You hear that, Enzo? Fox wants to *play.*" I grinned over at my friend.

Enzo handed me the joint and coughed through his laugh. "I don't even know where we're going with this."

I shrugged and inhaled the weed, enjoying the feeling as it flowed through my body. *Fuck, I needed the escape.* "I'm good with whatever. I assume our dicks are going to touch at some point. Not that I'm too keen on that. I just figure it can't be avoided."

"I figure so too." Fox sighed. "And I'm definitely not into any of you assholes that way. Even if I love you like brothers."

"I love you too, man."

"Same," Enzo said. "We just gotta get Ethan up and around now."

"Are you worried?" I peered over at Enzo, wondering if he'd show any signs of a chink in his well-placed armor. *Nothing.*

"I'm not. He's in good hands. I *was,* naturally. And yeah, I'm fucking nervous, but Ethan is strong. We've seen that over the years. I almost think the fucker might be invincible. Or is it immortal?"

"Immortal," Fox supplied. "He's been shot. He's overdosed. He's been beaten and left for dead multiple times. He's gotta be on his last life by now."

"Like a cat?" I laughed.

"Yeah, but he's definitely not a pussy." Enzo looked over at me and then back at Fox. "You fellas ready to get our boy back?"

"Hell, yeah," I said as Fox nodded.

"Let's do this shit. We can't be the four horsemen if we're down a man. Let's get Ethan's ass up."

And with those words, we piled out of the car and strode toward the hospital.

"ROBERT. JANIE." Enzo reached out and clasped Robert's hand before giving Janie a hug.

"Hey, guys," Robert greeted us. They were gathered outside of Ethan's room.

Ethan's adoptive parents were younger than the rest of our parents by a few years. Robert and Janie were barely into their forties if memory served me right. Ethan told us the story of how Robert had been adopted too, so he'd wanted to give someone else a good life. As far as people went, Robert and Janie were good ones. They'd been through so much with Ethan, but they never gave up on him.

"Hey, Robert. How are you guys?" I asked as Janie reached for me.

She was a slender woman with auburn curls. Robert was lucky in the female department. We always used to tease Ethan about how hot his mom was. He'd always laugh and shake his head while warning us she was off limits.

"Nervous," Janie said, breathing out and clutching her chest as she pulled away.

Robert's arm was immediately around her. "It'll be OK. Ethan's strong. The doctors are optimistic."

Janie gave us a wobbly smile. "How's Rosalie? I tried talking to her father in the cafeteria yesterday, but he didn't say much."

"That's because he's a prick," I said.

"Cole," Fox warned softly.

I shrugged. It wasn't a lie.

"She's about the same as Ethan. They're going to test her breathing today." Fox shot me a look to keep my mouth shut.

Robert shook his head. "I hate that they're struggling right now. This never should've happened. This is an absolute bunch of bullshit. That kid. . . Everything he did was to cause harm. He couldn't just off himself. He had to bring Ethan and Rosalie along for the ride. I'm not sad the piece of shit is gone."

"Robert," Janie admonished, her cheeks red. "Not here."

Robert glanced at Janie and then his gaze swiveled between me and Fox. "You boys did good."

"What?" Fox asked.

Robert looked away and didn't answer because the doctor came toward them.

"Robert. Janie," Doctor Browning said with a nod of his head. "Friends."

"Is it time?" Janie's small body shook, and Robert tightened his hold on her.

"It is. Based on everything we've seen with Ethan, I'm very optimistic about today. What's going to happen is my team and I are going to go in. His medications have been reduced already. I expect him to be coherent soon. As soon as he is, we'll start the extubation process with him."

"Can we go in?" Enzo asked, glancing at everyone.

"We don't like to have people in the room with us while we do this part. As long as it goes well, we'll be in and out in just a few moments. We want to make sure he's comfortable before letting anyone else in. Perhaps you could go visit your friend down the hall or grab an early lunch in the cafeteria."

"We're not leaving," Robert said immediately.

"I'm not either," I grunted.

I knew Rosalie would understand. She'd want us to be with Ethan. The guys nodded their agreement.

"Well, in that case, why don't you head down the hall and take a seat in the lounge. It could take us a bit, OK? We'll come get you the moment we have him breathing on his own."

We agreed, and Robert shook Doctor Browning's hand before we made our way to the waiting room.

I froze in the doorway when I saw Rosalie's parents sitting inside. I locked gazes with her father, the hatred sparking to life within me.

"Cole," Fox called out.

"Come. *Sit*," Enzo added.

Fuck that.

"I'm surprised you're here," I said loudly as I glared at her father. "Figured you would've pulled her plug and watched her and my baby die considering the shit you already put her through."

John rose to his feet and approached me. I clenched my hands into fists, ready to knock his fucking ass out.

This moment had been a long time coming.

CHAPTER 12

FOX

"Fuck." I was on my feet and between John and Cole in the span of a breath with Enzo right beside me.

"Don't get in my way," Cole snarled softly from behind me.

"Shut the fuck up, Cole," Enzo hissed back. "Don't do this shit. Rosalie wouldn't want you to fight her father."

"She's not here right now to tell me that, so it's a moot point," Cole snapped back.

Robert and Janie glanced at everyone, their faces pale. Cole needed to chill. If not for Rosie, then at least for Ethan's parents. We'd all been through hell.

"I don't know what sick things you *convinced* my daughter to do, but it's *over*," John said, glaring at Cole over my shoulder.

"Mr. Bishop, *John*, please. Not here. Cole is a little upset," I said, hoping to cool everyone down. I'd always gotten along with Rosalie's parents. The last thing we needed was for them to toss us out on our asses and not let us see her. "He cares for her. We all do."

John's gaze shot to me as Mrs. Bishop moved behind him and took his hand in hers. She shot me a worried look.

"Whatever sick relationship you *all* had with my daughter is done," John said dangerously. "Even you, Fox. You should've kept her safe, not led her into some disaster that ended with her in a fucking hospital bed needing a machine to breathe for her."

"You'll have to excuse me, *John*." Enzo drew himself up to his full height, one which towered over Rosalie's father. "But had you been a better father, our girl wouldn't be struggling to live in there. Neither would our baby. So you'll have to excuse us if we're a little pissed off right now. As her *father*, you should've been protecting her when she needed you instead of shoving her out into the street pregnant for the vultures to pick off."

John's face paled, and he drew in a deep breath. "I regret my actions, but my decision stands. Whatever was happening with you all is finished. You almost got her killed—"

"We saved her life." Cole shoved me hard to move me, but I held my ground and pushed him straight into the hallway. He glared up at me, his chest heaving.

"Not here, man. *Not fucking here*. All he has to do is say the word, and we're out. We won't get to see Rosalie. Keep your shit together," I seethed at him, my hands on either side of his face as he glared at me with wild, blue eyes. "Now take a deep breath and get your shit together. We'll walk it off." I released his face and pushed him back as he attempted to go in.

"Cole," I growled. "For Rosalie. For the baby. *Please*."

He stopped mid-shove and took a step back, a muscle feathering along his jaw.

"For my family," he whispered.

"Let's walk." I took him by the arm and steered him away from the lounge. I knew leaving Enzo behind would be fine. Enzo always knew what he had to do. I imagined he was in there either soothing wounds or creating more, but he'd do it with such style no one would question him once he was done.

Once we were in the parking lot, Cole exploded, his loud shout echoing around us.

I watched as he kicked a dumpster near a back entrance, his fingers tangled in his blond hair and his eyes wild.

"I killed for Rosalie and the baby. I fucking *took a life*, Fox," he huffed, sliding to his ass against the dumpster. "When I lie in bed at night, I still feel the vibration of his neck cracking in my hands. I still hear his sick, fucked up words in my head. I did it to protect the ones I love. I didn't do it so some prick could sit around and act like he has any fucking say in what *my* girl does, man. What the fuck?" He closed his eyes and rested his head against the dumpster.

"I know, man. I know, OK? You didn't do it in vain. Rosalie is his daughter. He cares about her just like you care about your baby."

"He kicked her out—"

"He acted irrationally. I'm sure he regrets those actions more than anything else in his life. This is a high-stress situation for everyone, but we need to be on one side only, and that's Rosalie's side. We need to make sure *she's* healthy, happy, and safe, even if we hate the people we're working with to make it happen. You're keeping your baby safe too, Cole." I slid down beside him against the dumpster and gave his knee a squeeze. He didn't say anything else, opting to keep his eyes closed, his lips turned down into a deep frown.

"Are you with me?" I whispered.

"I'm here," he answered softly. "I'm just worried." He opened his eyes and peered at me. "What if she's not the same when she wakes up? The doctors said she has a brain injury. I'm not stupid, man. I know what that can mean."

I swallowed and exhaled loudly. "I know. I'm worried too."

"What if everything has changed now? What if we really do lose and not because she decided she was over this shit, but because she can't even fucking remember who we are? That's a possibility, you know."

"It was a small brain bleed," I whispered, trying to tamp down my own anxiety. "Nominal, at best. The doctors said—"

"What if they're wrong? What if the girl in that bed already left us? She was fucking dead, Fox. *Dead.*"

"She wasn't dead that night," I said, the ugly memory of her struggling to breathe crashing into me.

"She was. You had to breathe for her."

"She's going to be OK, Cole. We need to believe that, man. If we don't, we'll all fall apart. Now isn't the time to lose your shit. I need you, OK? We *all* do. Let's just take it moment by moment. We can't keep lashing out and fucking off. It's too much drama. I can't take much more."

Cole blew out a breath. "You're right. I'm sorry."

"It's OK. I'm sorry too."

"What are *you* sorry for?" He scoffed.

"I feel guilty because it's my fault. I thought I was doing the right thing by doing Juliet's bidding to keep Rosie safe. I'd planned on telling Rosie everything, but then I just got so caught up in her wanting *me*—us—that I lost track of shit. When Juliet came at me with everything, I felt blindsided and desperate. I fucked up. Bad. I only wanted to protect Rosie. Now look. She's fighting for hers and the baby's lives."

"We'll take care of Juliet. You read Rosalie's answer in the note-book. She wants us. I mean, I hope she still does, but it's the one piece of hope I'm going to cling to. I want us to be happy together. I dream of it."

"Me too," I murmured.

We sat in silence for nearly an hour, both of us staring off in the distance. I imagined he was running scenarios through his head just like I was.

"Hey," Enzo called out as he approached. He had his dark aviators in place.

We both stared at him as he stopped in front of us.

"You two done holding each other's dicks?"

"Why? Jealous?" Cole sighed and gave him a tired smile.

Enzo flashed his million-watt grin. "Maybe. We've got more important things to talk about though."

I leaned forward, my heart banging hard. "Ethan—"

"He's awake."

"He is?" Cole was on his feet in seconds, me following.

"Yeah. And he's asking for us. Now, you two assholes done fucking around, or do you need me to kick your ass to get your head in the game?"

"Let's go," I said, stepping around Enzo, eager to get to Ethan.

"Hey, Fox," Enzo called out.

I stopped and turned to face him.

"All in? Together?"

"There's nothing I want more."

"Let's do this shit then." Enzo grinned and clapped me on the shoulder as Cole gave me a knowing smile.

All in. Now, we had to get our fourth.

CHAPTER 13

My head felt like a sledgehammer had been taken to it. My chest felt worse.

"Get this shit out of me," I grunted, gesturing to the tube stuffed up my cock so I could piss. "I swear if you don't take it out, I'll do it my damn self."

"Ethan, honey, calm down. Let the nurse do her job," my mom said from beside me, patting my hand in a soothing way.

Dad hovered in the corner. After I'd woken up and was able to tell the doctor my name and answer his other foolish questions, they'd let my parents in. The waterworks started as soon as they'd laid eyes on me.

No one would answer my questions though. I finally demanded to see Fox, Cole and Enzo. They'd be straight with me.

"Easy," the nurse said as I fidgeted again. Young. Beautiful. She had nothing on my sweetheart though.

My mind was wild as I thought about Rosalie. Vague memories of Enzo and Fox's voices telling me she was nearby had me chomping at the bit to find her and hold her.

"Listen," I started again, more calmly this time.

I was so fucking groggy. But I shoved it all aside, forcing myself to be more coherent. I was an addict for fuck's sake. If there was one thing I knew how to do, it was how to get my shit together to be coherent and functioning. "I hurt. I want to see my girlfriend. I want to see my friends. Can you please have this thing removed? I'll piss in a jug if I need to, but this shit needs to go."

"Doctor Browning stepped out to check on another patient. As soon as he's done, I'll ask him about removing the catheter, OK? We just don't want to have to reinsert it later if something pops up."

"The only thing that's going to pop up is my damn anger, Nurse…"

"I'm Jasmine. I'm going to need you to try to relax. You've been injured pretty bad—"

"Get me some pain meds," I grumbled, wincing.

A look of concern filled my dad's eyes.

My chest ached. My throat felt like razors had played hopscotch inside it. And my wrists were fucked. The pain ebbed from my shoulders to my fingertips. The ugly white bandages served as a reminder of what that prick had done to me. *When I get my hands on Ian. . .*

"I need some water too," I croaked as Jasmine adjusted my IV's. "My throat feels like it's on fire."

"Ah, Mr. Masters, it's good to see you still awake," my doctor proclaimed with a smile on his face, crinkling the corners of his eyes. He exchanged handshakes with my parents.

"So how are you feeling?"

"Like there's a drumline practicing in my head," I answered in a raspy voice. "My whole body hurts. I-I need something."

Doctor Browning nodded at Jasmine. "I put an order in for some pain medication."

"I'll be right back," she said, stepping out of the room.

"So… You were in an accident," Doctor Browning started.

"I recall."

"The police are probably going to want to get a statement from you, but I informed them you'll need some time to really wake up."

"Where's my girlfriend? Rosalie Bishop. Is she OK?" To hell with the cops. I needed Rosalie.

Doctor Browning pulled up a stool and sat down beside me. He shared a look with my parents. "Hospital policy doesn't allow me to discuss other patients with anyone but their next of kin."

I started to protest, making the heart monitor beep more wildly.

The doctor held up his hand. "Even though I can't share any information with you, I'm pretty sure your parents can probably shed some light on things for you." He shot them a knowing look.

I settled back down and turned to my parents. "Where's Rosalie?"

"She's down the hall. Sleeping still. She…" Mom's voice broke.

Dad took over for her. "Son, her injuries were more severe than yours."

Tears welled in my own eyes. "And the baby?" I whispered, worry coursing through me.

"The baby's OK as far as they know. But they're taking things day by day," Dad explained.

"Does that mean she could lose the baby still?" Nausea churned my guts. *My poor sweetheart.* I needed to get to her.

"Anything can happen, and like I said, Rosalie is far worse off than you."

"Meaning?" My chest ached. I wanted to rub it, but my wrists were killing me.

"Rosalie was in a car accident. She has some injuries that require a little more time to heal."

A tear trickled down my cheek at my dad's words, the uncertainty in his tone, and the silence emanating from the doctor. I wanted to demand more answers. But my tears were my mother's undoing.

"Ethan," she whispered, reaching out a shaky hand and pushing my hair away from my forehead. "Oh, honey!"

"Don't cry, Mom," I croaked.

"We've just been so worried, Son," Dad said in a choked voice, a sheen of tears in his own eyes.

"I'm fine," I hurried to assure them, wincing as my throat burned.

"Here." Doctor Browning handed me a styrofoam cup of water with a straw. "Drink slowly."

I drank it down greedily, enjoying the way the coolness helped to quell the fire. He took my empty cup from me and returned to his stool.

"How are you really feeling?" Mom asked, her eyes filled with worry.

"A bit like I've been shot in my chest," I answered. "But the pain reminds me I'm still alive."

"Can you give him something? I mean, with his history," Dad started, giving me an apologetic look. I knew he was worried when I'd asked for something earlier.

"We're going to. With Ethan's history, we're going to go for some low dose pain medications and see how that works. We want him to be comfortable, but we don't want to have bigger issues later on."

"I'm here to tell you right now, I'll get help if I need it. Just. . .*anything* right now. I hurt." I wasn't milking it. The pain made me want to vomit.

"Is there anything else you can do for pain management? I mean, I'm worried about the potential for long term issues ... but I can't stand seeing him in this kind of pain," Mom said.

Even though everything hurt like a bitch, I wanted to ease her concerns. "I can handle it," I promised.

Doctor Browning nodded. "Jasmine will be back shortly with your medication."

Just as he finished his sentence, she came into the room. She moved to my IV and inserted a needle. A rush of warmth hit me a moment later. I relaxed deeper into my bed and let out a sigh.

Fuck me, that hit the spot.

"How's that?" Doctor Browning asked.

"I'm good," I mumbled, my eyelids heavy. "I want to see Rosalie. I want to see my friends."

"You will. But we need you to rest up, OK?" Doctor Browning patted my hand gently. "You're a hell of a fighter, kid. Hell of a fighter. I'll be back later after my rounds to check on you again. If you need anything, use your call button."

And with that, he left the room, taking Nurse Jasmine with him.

"I'm sorry," I started groggily. "I didn't mean for this to happen—"

"We know, Ethan. It's OK," Mom murmured, running her fingers gently through my hair.

"You guys won't be able to afford the hospital bill. I-I'll sell more photographs and get a second, even third, job to help—"

"Don't worry about it, Ethan. We'll figure it out. We can remortgage the house," Dad said. "Or take out a loan."

My eyes burned with the threat of tears. "I don't want you to do that. It's too much. I'll pay for the bill myself—"

"Honey, don't worry about it, OK? Dad and I will take care of it. We just want you better. Jace and Emma miss you so much." Mom sniffled.

"I miss them too," I mumbled sleepily. "I've caused you guys so many problems—"

"You've been a great son, Ethan. Don't start thinking otherwise. We love you." Dad reached down and rested his hand over mine. "When we thought we lost you, our whole world came crumbling down," his voice cracked, and he wiped at a tear. "Just get better for us. That's all we want."

"I will. I promise," I said softly.

"You ready to see your friends? They've been here pretty much every day. Enzo is in the lounge right now. I can get him."

"Please. I-I want Cole and Fox too."

"OK, honey." Mom placed a kiss on my forehead and left the room.

"Dad?"

"Yeah?"

"Is Ian here?" I wanted to kick his ass. Putting a bullet in his chest seemed like the best idea, really. The piece of shit didn't deserve to draw breath. Ugly scenes from that night flooded my mind, and I gave a shudder.

"No. Ian. . . he passed away." Dad didn't look the least bit upset at the information.

My heart thudded hard in my chest.

"How?"

"Car accident they say. Cole and Fox found his car wrapped

around a tree with him and Rosalie inside. They tried to save him. Fox pulled him from the fire—"

"It was on f-fire?" my voice shook at the information.

Dad nodded. "Yeah. Ian didn't survive his injuries. Fox performed CPR until help arrived to save Rosalie. She's banged up pretty bad."

"Sweetheart," I whispered, a tear slipping from the corner of my eye.

"The guys will tell you more, I'm sure. Rosalie's mom has been keeping Fox updated."

I closed my eyes, trying to shove the ugly images of Ian on top of her out of my head. It was the shit nightmares were made of.

"Ethan," Dad called out softly.

"Mm?"

"Enzo told us about, uh, you guys."

"I love her. I love them, Dad. I always will. They're like brothers to me. It's that simple."

He patted my hand gently again. "OK. We only want your happiness."

"They're my happiness."

"Then that's all that matters."

The conversation ended because Enzo, Cole, and Fox came into the room. Dad got to his feet and stepped away.

"Your mom and I will be back later. We'll see about getting you some food, OK?"

"Thanks, Dad," I whispered, watching him lead Mom out.

I shifted my swimming vision to the guys.

"Hey, dicks," I greeted them in my soft, raspy voice.

"Hey, you immortal son of a bitch," Enzo returned, grinning.

"Get over here," I called out, the smile making my face hurt.

The guys came to my side. Enzo reached me first. He pressed his warm lips to my forehead.

"I thought we'd lost you, E. I've never been so scared in my entire life."

"You saved me, man. I owe you a lot."

"You don't owe me shit but a promise to get out of this bed and join us."

"Done." I laughed softly as he backed away.

Fox was next. "I don't even have words. I'm just so glad you're back. I love you, Ethan."

"So I've heard," I chuckled, recalling his words from when I was under. "I fucking love you too, Fox."

He grinned at me. I looked to Cole.

"You look like shit, bro."

I gave him a tired smile. "So do you, asshole. What's got your panties in a twist?"

"Your crazy ass. I've been worried sick about you."

"Prove it," I challenged, struggling to keep my eyes open.

He approached my bedside and pressed a kiss to my forehead and rested his head against mine.

"Are you crying?" I whispered.

"Fuck you, Ethan," Cole sniffled. "I fucking love you, man."

"I love you too. I'd love you more if you brought me something to eat."

He laughed softly and backed away. "I have a fruit basket for you, but I forgot to bring it."

"Well, shit," I muttered. "Does it at least have strawberries?"

"You know it, man."

"Nice. Bring it tomorrow."

"I will."

The guys shuffled around, pulling two chairs up, one on either side of my bed. Enzo took a seat near my feet at the end of the bed.

"Tell me about Rosalie," I demanded.

Fox cleared his throat. "She's been in a medically induced coma since she arrived, like you. They ran some tests today to see if they could wean her off the ventilator and wake her up... Her breathing wasn't strong enough to take her off just yet, but they're going to try again soon. The bleeding she had on her brain has stopped, so they aren't going to have to operate at this point." Fox's voice was thick with emotion.

"Fuck," I choked out, my chest aching for a whole slew of new reasons. "What else?"

"Ian cut her up pretty bad, so she had to get some stitches. Almost all the ribs on her left side are broken or fractured. She has a fractured leg and arm. And she suffered some burns in the accident. But they weren't super serious since Cole and Fox got her out in time. They're mostly on her feet and legs. First and second degree. She needs help breathing, so she's been on a ventilator for a few days. They've been trying to wean her off, like Fox said, but some days seem to be better than others," Enzo gazed out the window as he spoke.

I wanted to scream. I wanted to fucking bring Ian back from the dead and kill his ass all over again. That useless son of a bitch!

Fox reached out and wiped my eyes for me with a tissue and offered me a sad smile. I looked over to see the photo of her in a purple sundress, smiling.

My sweetheart.

"Which one of you killed Ian?" I whispered.

The guys looked at one another. I didn't think they'd answer me until Cole spoke up.

"Me."

"How did you do it?" I asked thickly, desperate to know.

"I broke his neck."

I nodded, my throat tight. "Good."

"They think it happened in the accident. No one knows," Cole continued softly.

"And no one ever will." I leveled my tired eyes on Cole.

He smirked. "I'm only getting started."

I shifted my gaze to Fox who frowned and then to Enzo who gave me a quick smile.

"Whatever you're planning, I want to help."

"Didn't doubt you for a minute," Enzo said. "Welcome back."

"It's good to be back," I answered. "Now, let's get our girl to join us."

CHAPTER 14

FOX

"The Bishops are on their way," I said quietly, looking to Enzo. "Her mom just texted me."

I didn't need to explain to Enzo what that meant. We needed to make sure Cole was kept away. Keeping the peace was important. Being able to continue to visit her and get updates from her parents was vital to our sanity. Plus, I didn't know what Rosie had planned, but I didn't want any of us to fuck up anything for her.

"Cole, you should take Ethan his fruit basket. I'll go with you." Enzo's dark eyes took in Cole whose mouth was drawn into a deep frown.

I was just about to clear my throat to get Cole moving when he got to his feet before leaning down and placing a kiss on Rosalie's temple. We'd been sitting with her all morning, and only by the grace of Mrs. Bishop's patience were we able to stay to see her. It appeared John had been pissed about her overruling him, but she'd stood up to him.

"I love you, Rosebud. I'll be back later," Cole whispered. "Please be here when I get back. Keep our blossom safe."

My guts twisted at his soft, desperate words. Silently, I watched as he moved lower and leaned over her abdomen, giving it a tender kiss. His hand rested just below where he'd placed his lips.

"Daddy loves you, Blossom. I'll be back tomorrow." He didn't move except for his slow, deep breathing and his thumb making gentle circles on the cotton fabric of her hospital gown.

Fuck.

If I had any doubts about Cole, they ended in that moment. I locked eyes with Enzo who gave me a slight nod, acknowledging the same thing I had.

Cole would be OK. We just needed to keep him sane until Rosie woke up. Each of us had a little piece inside us that only she could calm. We were a tangled, fucking mess without her. My worry was Cole would lose his shit, and we'd never get him back. I knew he and Enzo were up to something, but deep down, I didn't even want to think about it. I had shit with Juliet to sort out, and I just needed my Rosie back to soothe the ache in my heart.

After they left, I stayed with Rosie, holding her hand. I wasn't sure what the fuck I was going to do. All I knew was I had this deep fucking trench in my heart only she could fill. I'd do anything for her, even go back to Juliet if it meant Rosie would be safe from Juliet's vicious plans for just a little while longer. Even though I'd agreed with Enzo earlier, I was desperate for Rosalie to tell me what I should do. I meant what I'd said when I said I'd let her make the choice. I wanted shit out in the open.

I'd even let her read all the messages from Juliet on my phone if she needed to.

I reached out and grabbed my notebook. I released Rosie's hand to take my pencil. Frustration was my new friend. I clenched my teeth as I scratched words onto the notebook paper.

I had to get this shit out of my head. Without Rosalie to talk to, all I had was the paper, so there I sat, scribbling furiously in my own notebook. It was a diary of stories I'd kept since I was a kid. Or at least one of many. I'd filled countless notebooks with poetry, songs, and stories over the years, most of them involving a beautiful, fiery-maned girl who I just couldn't get out of my head or my heart, the years between be damned.

The soft beeping of the monitor sounded out around us as I wrote the story of our first kiss. Whenever she woke up from this current hell, I had every intention of telling her how I'd felt when we were kids. About how much that innocent kiss had meant to me. Then I'd tell her about the first time I'd kissed her when we were older and what it had done to my heart. I just wanted to make sure I had the right words for when that moment came. Even if she changed her mind about everything, I needed her to know.

"Hello, Fox," Mrs. Bishop called out softly as she and her husband stepped into the room. She went to Rosalie's side and kissed her forehead. "How was she this afternoon?"

"Good." I snapped my notebook closed and glanced at Rosie's dad as he stood at the foot of her bed. I was positive his guilt was eating him alive. I'd always liked him. Stern. Strict. No-nonsense . . .but a decent man who'd made some bad decisions.

Join the fucking club.

I turned my attention back to Mrs. Bishop as she stared down at Rosalie, tears in her eyes.

"She looks so pale," she murmured. "And I hate the sound that machine makes."

"That machine is keeping her alive," Cole's voice called out as he stepped into the room.

Fuck.

Enzo must have lost track of him.

"Cole," I growled, rising from my seat and going to him as Rosie's mom opened her mouth in surprise. "*Not* here. Not now. Not again. *Please*, man."

"No, let him say his piece," Mr. Bishop finally said, drawing himself up to his impressive height. "I'm interested in what he has to say. Our conversation was cut short last time."

"Mr. Bishop, I really don't think now is the best time. Rosie—"

"Rosalie is having my baby. When she wakes up and gets released, I'm taking her with me. As far as I'm concerned, you can go to hell. You're the reason she's lying in this fucking bed in the first place, you asshole."

I thought Mr. Bishop would launch himself across the room at Cole.

Instead, he nodded. "You can't make me feel worse than I already do. You're right. A lot of this is my fault. I wasn't the greatest father to her. I never listened to her troubles or encouraged her in the things she loved. I even *denied* her those things, and because of it, *this* happened. You can blame me. I accept that. I know I pushed her out when she needed us the most. If she'll ever even speak to me again, it'll be a miracle. If she loses her b-baby. . ." his voice cracked, and his eyes misted over. "Well, I'll blame myself for that too."

Cole glared at him for a moment before tearing his gaze away and peering at Rosalie. His bottom lip trembled. "I'll *never* let anyone hurt her again. Ever. That includes you."

The silence in the room was palpable. I rested my hand on Cole's shoulder.

"We should go, so Rosie's parents can spend some time with her," I murmured.

Cole nodded tightly before moving to Rosie and bending down. He whispered something in her ear I couldn't hear before kissing her cheek and stepping away. I watched his back as he left the room before I leaned over to kiss Rosalie too.

"I love you, baby. I hope we get to talk tomorrow. I'll dream of you tonight." I backed away and gave her parents a nod before disappearing from the room.

Cole leaned against the wall outside, a muscle thrumming along his jaw.

"What the fuck, man? Really? You needed to do that shit here? Tonight? *Again?* We talked about this!"

He didn't say anything, only shook his head and let out a scoff.

Enzo joined us in the hall. "I'd ask where you went, but judging by how the fuck this looks, I don't need two guesses."

"He decided he wanted to confront Rosie's dad in her room... *again*. Nice, huh?" I shot a sour look at Cole.

"I'm leaving," he grunted, storming away from us.

Enzo and I exchanged quick looks before jogging after him into the elevator. I ground my teeth as Cole pulled out his phone and texted someone.

"You can't be doing that shit, Cole. Especially not in Rosalie's room," I started. "Everything is a fucking mess right now, and that shit isn't helping. They could stop us from seeing her. They could decide not to tell us what's going on. Is that what you want?"

The elevator doors opened, and Cole stormed out. We followed him outside.

"Fucking say something! Don't just walk away—" I reached out and grabbed his arm.

He spun and threw a punch, landing it hard on my cheek. I let out a snarl and shoved him. Enzo was between us within seconds.

"You don't know what the fuck it's like," Cole rasped, breathing hard. "Rosalie is having my baby. *My* kid! I don't want any mother fucker causing her an ounce of pain. I'll fucking kill someone. Again." His chest heaved as he glared at me.

"I understand," I said softly.

"You fucking don't. You *just fucking* don't." A tear leaked down his cheek, his bottom lip trembling. "I have a chance to have a family with a girl I'm head over heels for. I *can't* lose that. I won't. It doesn't matter who it is that gets in the way. I won't allow it. I-I killed for her. I fucking ended someone's life for her. Do you understand how fucking deep I am in with her? With our baby? I don't give a shit if that's her old man up there in my way. I'll fucking end him too."

"Easy, man," Enzo said gently. "We know. We get it."

Cole's Adam's apple bobbed as he shook his head. "I'm sorry. This entire thing has made me insane. I'm barely holding on here. It makes it worse that I have no idea what version of Rosebud is going to wake up. Will it be the one who still wants us? Will she hate me for leaving? What if she doesn't want *me* anymore? I know I sound nuts, but man, it's a big possibility. Ian fucked her up. You know he did."

"She's going to want you, Cole. For fuck's sake, you're the father of her kid. She wanted you before this. She'll want you after. Worrying about it won't change a damn thing except make you feel out of control, and we don't need that shit from you right now. OK?

Tomorrow is a new day. They're going to take Rosalie off the machines. Her testing went well today. We might be talking to her by this time tomorrow. Just focus on that and not the other shit," I said.

Cole nodded. "Fine. I'll try."

"Come stay at my place tonight," Enzo murmured, reaching out for Cole and pulling him in for a one-armed hug. "We can unwind. I'll talk to my dad. If he's cool with it, and I think he will be, we can start getting things for the guest house. It's a little on the bare side right now since we don't use it. And the beds are shitty." Enzo glanced over his shoulder at me as he released Cole. "You too, Fox."

"I'm in. And I really want to see what the fuck an Alaskan king bed is."

Enzo grinned and winked at me. "You're going to love it."

CHAPTER 15

ENZO

After a long night of arguing over everything from which color comforter Rosalie would prefer to leather reclining couch versus a pull-out sofa, we finally settled down in my bedroom to sleep.

"What the fuck are you doing?" Cole called out as Fox grabbed a sleeping bag from my closet.

"Getting ready for bed?"

"Listen, I don't know if I punched you in the face too hard earlier, but let's take a minute to think this over. We're all going to be sleeping in the same bed at some point, right?"

"I'm not going to let you spoon me, fuck face," Fox snorted.

Shaking my head at their banter, I glanced at them from where I sat at my desk trying to find sheets that would fit the big ass bed I'd ordered a few minutes ago. Cole snatched the sleeping bag from him and chucked it back into the closet.

"Then let Enzo, dick wad. But don't you think we should get used to it? I know I'm not planning to let her sleep alone."

"She won't be alone," I called out. "I'll be there."

Cole shot a triumphant look at Fox. "See? Enzo knows what's up."

89

"I do," I added, enjoying the look on Fox's face. "Should I get you some sexy underwear while I'm buying sheets?" I smirked at him.

"Yeah, make 'em fucking pink and lacy, asshole." Fox stomped over to my bed.

I hid the smile on my face as he tugged the covers back and crawled into my king size. With a low growl, he settled in.

"Don't grab my ass, Scott. I'll return that fucking cheek check you gave me earlier."

"Like I'd want your ass, Evans. I'd fucking break you."

Fox shot him the finger without turning over to look at him. I chuckled at their exchange. We were *almost* back to normal with two exceptions.

Ethan and Rosalie.

We'd have them with us soon. I knew we would. Ethan had slept most of the day. Personally, I thought he had too many pain medications, but I was no doctor, and I knew he was in pain, so I let it slide. The bitch of the situation would come later when it was time to get him off the meds. Not a feat I looked forward to.

When I'd shared my concerns with Fox and Cole, they'd agreed. Both were worried about how this shit would go down. It wasn't like we were brand new to the subject of Ethan's drug use and depression.

My attention was drawn back to Cole who was sliding into bed next to Fox, a mischievous grin on his face. I smirked, knowing what Cole was up to.

Fox let out a squeal as Cole sidled up behind him and wrapped him in a bear hug before finger blasting his belly button. I couldn't stop my laughter as Fox fell out of bed and landed on his ass. Cole snickered so loudly I was sure my father's men downstairs could hear him.

"Asshole," Fox grumbled, getting to his feet and shooting a half-assed annoyed look at Cole. But there was relief in the look.

I knew what he was thinking. Cole would be OK as long as we could keep his mind off shit.

Fox slid back beneath the covers and turned to face Cole. "I'll shave your fucking eyebrows off, man, if you do that shit again."

Cole snorted and shook his head before settling against his pillow, leaving a good six inches between them.

Quickly, I added a pair of large, pink, lacy panties for Fox as a joke to my online cart and checked out, before shutting down my computer and turning off the lights. I got into bed beside Cole.

"You should sleep in the middle. You're less likely to grab my ass," Fox grumbled from his side.

"I'll do just about anything for twenty bucks, Evans. And that includes grabbing your ass," I said, burrowing beneath my sheets and letting out a contented sigh. It had been a long day. Sleep was a welcomed reward.

Fox grumbled something incoherent which made me and Cole laugh.

"It's going to be OK, right?" Cole mumbled softly into the darkness a moment later.

"It will be," I assured him.

The mattress shifted on the other side of Cole. Fox must have rolled onto his back.

"We have Juliet to deal with. And I guess we'll know more once we hear from Rosalie," Fox murmured.

"Fuck Juliet," I grumbled. "Let her make her move. We can certainly handle a fucking cheerleader." I still hadn't told Fox about my current role in the matter as assigned by my father.

Fox was always trying to quell the waves within Cole. He didn't need to break his ass to do it with me too. This was my life. I was a mobster's son. I wanted this now. I needed the control. To be in charge. The entire situation which had left me feeling helpless had ultimately led me to feeling powerful. *To being powerful.* I couldn't let it go for anything. I wanted to take down anyone who crossed me. I'd been far too nice for way too long. That shit was over now. It had taken me the last few days to come to that conclusion. I didn't have an out. I never did. Thinking otherwise was foolish.

"Then we should get this shit over with." Cole let out a soft, bitter laugh.

"You know what I told you," I said. "We have a plan. Let's stick to it."

"I could always just go back to Juliet," Fox mumbled, ignoring my comment. "I'd do it if it meant keeping her off everyone else's asses, especially Rosalie's."

"And we talked about that already," I pointed out. "It's stupid."

"You know where I stand." Cole's voice came out with a hard edge. "All she has to do is make *one* wrong move. I won't fucking hesitate."

"We should sleep." Fox shifted again. "We have a long day tomorrow with Rosalie. Oh, and Ethan wants us to grab him more fruit too."

"I got him another basket in my car." Cole sighed. "He's a freak of nature with his fruit obsession."

"He told me that at one time it was the only thing he could steal to eat," I said softly. "I think it's a comfort and control thing for him."

Cole shook his head. "Poor fucked up bastard."

"He's gotten a lot better." Fox paused. "Did you guys see the scars on his legs today when they tried getting him out of bed?"

"Yeah. I didn't know it had gotten that bad," I said into the darkness.

"He'll be fine. He's made it this long." Cole tugged the blankets closer.

"I think he'll be fine too. He might need some help, but that's what we're for."

The blankets shifted back down the bed.

"Listen, Fox, I need to be fully covered at night. None of this kicking blankets shit," Cole grumbled.

"I hate being hot," Fox complained. "Why the hell do you have thirty fucking blankets on your bed, Enzo?"

"There are two," I called out. "And a sheet. These blankets cost more than your wardrobe, Evans. Be gentle."

"Eat me, De Luca."

I laughed.

"I'm going to have to get my own damn blanket. Enzo, come on, dude. Why are you taco-ing into this shit like an Italian burrito?" Cole tugged uselessly on the blanket and let out a sigh.

"My bed. My rules."

Cole punched his pillow and grumbled, "I don't think the Alaskan king bed is going to be big enough."

"It'll get way hotter in here once Rosalie and Ethan join us. Best get used to it, fellas. But I'll do some research to see if there's a bigger option." I released some of my blanket, and Cole immediately tugged it to himself.

"Dibs on sleeping next to Rosie," Fox called out with a yawn.

"Fuck you, Evans. Rosebud is sleeping next to me."

"I've loved her longer. Seniority rules," Fox argued.

"She's having my baby."

"Shut up, you assholes. My bed. My rules, remember? I'll get her first." I grinned as they argued, citing reasons why they should be able to hold her at night.

"But speaking of the baby, we're going to need a nursery," Cole said softly.

"We can set up a crib in the corner of the second bedroom. Let that room technically be Rosalie's and the baby's," I suggested, picturing the logistics.

"And I'll stay in there with her and the baby," Cole said smugly.

"No, we'll *all* take turns helping her with the baby because we're in this together, one big happy family. Besides, she's not due until summer, and we'll be leaving for college soon after the baby is born," Fox was quick to correct him.

"So the baby won't need anything too elaborate in the guest house then. And when we look for a place close to the college, we'll make sure to get a place big enough that everyone can have some private space to escape to, plus a nursery, and a room for our big ass family bed," I said, thrilled to be making decisions in the best interest of my family.

The room finally grew silent. I heard Fox's deep breathing as he fell under. Cole soon followed suit. I shifted so I could grab my phone off the dresser and opened it to my gallery where I looked at a photo of Rosalie and Ethan. They didn't know I'd taken the photo of them. They were in the hallway at school. Ethan held her close when they thought no one was around. It was right before Ethan left for rehab. But I was Lorenzo De Luca. I was around that day. I was every-fuck-ing-where.

Soon enough, everyone would know what I was capable of.

I smiled down at the image.

Tomorrow couldn't come fast enough. I needed them back. We had work to do.

CHAPTER 16

FOX

I breathed out and stretched my neck as I stood outside Ethan's door with Enzo and Cole. Ethan's parents were inside with the doctor, going over the details of his pending release. It was a tentative plan, but it made us all breathe out a sigh of relief.

Enzo rubbed the scruff on his face as he stared down at a photo of Ethan and Rosalie on his phone.

"When did you take that?" I asked, looking down at the picture.

"Few weeks ago when no one was looking," he mumbled.

In the photo, Ethan had his forehead resting against Rosie's. They held one another, worry on their faces. Ethan had told us Juliet found him and Rosie together. This must have been that day because they were risking a lot being together in the middle of the hallway.

"She looks beautiful," I murmured.

"She always does. My sunshine on a cloudy day," Enzo returned. "Do you want a copy?"

"Yeah. Send it."

Enzo tapped on his screen, and my phone buzzed. Before I could open it, the door to Ethan's room opened, and the doctor stepped out.

"Is he being released?" Cole demanded.

"Things are looking good." Doctor Browning smiled. "If things continue to progress, I don't see why we can't let him out of here by the end of the week."

"Hell yeah." I high-fived Cole.

"Can we see him?" Enzo asked.

"He's with his parents right now. It's up to them."

I nodded to the guys. "Let's give him some time with them."

"And Rosalie?" Cole asked. "Will she be coming off the machines today?"

"You know I'm not a liberty to discuss her condition. But I will say things are looking better."

"Mrs. Bishop left me a voicemail this morning. She said everything went well last night as they started weaning Rosie off things. They're going to try to take her off the vent today," I said.

"That's the plan," Doctor Browning said, glancing at his watch. "Matter of fact, I'm due in her room in a few minutes."

"We'll be waiting to hear the good news," I said, forcing confidence in my words.He gave me a wink. "I'll send someone to find you once we have some news. Hang tight, OK?"

I nodded and watched him walk away.

"She's going to be awake soon." Enzo glanced between me and Cole.

"Dibs on holding her first," I said.

Cole scoffed. "Like hell. I'll punch you again."

I grinned at him. "Then we should probably step outside now. I'll fight back this time."

"I'd expect nothing less." And he smirked back at me.

"Hey, E," Enzo greeted Ethan.

Ethan's face brightened, and he pushed his empty pudding cup away. "Hey, guys. I was wondering when you'd get here. I would've texted, but my damn wrists hurt. Eating that pudding nearly took my ass out."

"Need me to feed you a banana?" Cole offered with a playful grin as he held up the fruit basket.

"Sounds kinky. I'll bite," Ethan joked.

Cole chuckled and opened the basket, pulling out a banana. I sat down in the seat next to Ethan's bed while Enzo grabbed the chair on the opposite side. Cole sank down onto the spot next to Ethan's torso on the bed and offered him the banana.

"You're going to feed me?" Ethan lifted a dark brow and smirked at Cole.

"Open your mouth, hot stuff."

Ethan chuckled but obeyed, biting off a large portion and chewing slowly.

"Fuck, that's good. I hate pudding."

"How the fuck can you hate pudding?" Enzo asked, looking bewildered. "It's literally the best shit in the world."

"*This* shit is butterscotch, making it worse. I loathe butterscotch." Ethan nodded to his empty container and opened his mouth.

Cole put the banana inside Ethan's mouth, and he bit down again.

"How'd you sleep?" I asked.

"Surprisingly well. This bed sucks, but I guess I shouldn't expect much for the hundred-thousand-dollar hospital bill my parents are going to have." His good mood dissipated.

"No worries, E. I have it on good authority the bill won't be an issue."

Ethan frowned at Enzo. "What did you do?"

Enzo held his hands up and smiled. "Nothing."

Ethan shook his head and gazed back at me. "They said I might be able to leave tomorrow."

"We heard. That's awesome, man."

"Yeah, my parents said I can come stay with them while I recover—"

"Actually," Enzo cut in as Cole offered Ethan more banana.

Ethan took the final bite and chewed, his eyes focused on Enzo.

"My parents gave me the guest house on the back of the property. I was thinking you'd join us."

"What? You guys are all moving in together?" Ethan looked between us, his eyes wide.

"Well, I'll be in and out," I said, clearing my throat. "I can't leave my dad all alone, but I'll be there most nights since he works out of town a lot. As much as I want to move out, I don't think my dad is ready for that yet. With Mom being gone, I don't know that he'd be OK."

Cole shot me a sad smile but nodded. "It's cool, man. More Rosalie for us."

"I still get to hold her first. And I'm sure she'll be happy to give me my fill."

"Whatever." Cole rolled his eyes.

I knew he was still stupid nervous about how things would go down when she finally woke up.

"I ordered us an Ace family sized bed. It's bigger than an Alaskan king. Figured it would keep weird spooning to a minimum and give everyone a little breathing room," Enzo continued. "Should be here later in the week. I got an Alaskan king for the second bedroom too. I figured Rosalie might need some space of her own. We'll put the crib in there with her. For now though, each bedroom has a bed in it, and there's a couch which pulls out into a bed."

"I'm in. I don't want to burden my parents more. Plus, I think Jace and Emma might be scared to see me like this. I don't want that ugly memory in their heads."

"Awesome." Enzo leaned back in his seat. "It's settled then."

"And Rosalie?" Ethan called out.

We all glanced at one another.

"I want her with us. With Enzo at his place," I said. "It's really the best place for her with all this shit going on. I know her parents want her home, but I think it'll be a shit show. She's eighteen. She can decide for herself."

"I just hope she decides on us," Cole said softly, dropping the banana peel on the bedside tray.

"I just want her to wake up. I fucking miss her." Ethan closed his eyes for a moment. "Can you guys come get me when she wakes up? I want to see her."

"Of course," Enzo said. "They're working on it right now, actually."

Ethan peered at the door, his Adam's apple bobbing. "What will we do if she never gets better?"

"She *will*," I announced fiercely, not wanting to contemplate for a moment any other outcome.

Ethan fixed his gaze on me. "Promise?"

"Cross my heart."

Because fuck, I'd die with her.

CHAPTER 17

When Ethan fell asleep on us, we headed to the cafeteria to grab some food. I was halfway through my cheeseburger when Fox's phone vibrated with a message.

We all stared at him as he read the text, his eyes shimmering with moisture.

"She's awake," he whispered.

I dropped my burger and shoved my tray away.

"Stay here." Fox got to his feet and grabbed his tray.

"Stay here? Fuck you. *You* stay here," I snapped, getting to my feet.

Fox let out a sigh, a muscle thrumming along his jaw. "They asked for me, OK? Her mom said she's not really coherent yet but was calling my name. Just. . .let me do this. I swear you'll be able to see her soon."

Enzo's warm hand clamped down on my shoulder. "Go, Fox. We'll wait. Text us, OK?"

Fox shot me a pained look before spinning on his heel and leaving.

"This is bullshit." I blew out a breath as I glared at the doors Fox had disappeared through.

"Fox and Rosalie have a long history. Plus, her dad can't stand your ass. Let this play out slowly, their way. We want her when she's ready to go home. The more you piss her parents off, the further you push our chances of that away."

"You're going to blame *me*?" I demanded, leveling my scowl on him.

Enzo held up his hands in surrender. "I'm not, man. I'm saying that's what will play out if you push. Just relax. Fox will take care of her. He'll let us know what's going on. She's probably totally out of it anyway. Finish your lunch. We'll hit up the gift shop and get her and the baby something."

I let the tension leave my shoulders and sat back in my seat. We finished eating in silence before heading to the gift shop. I knew Ethan would have trouble texting back because of the damage to tendons and shit in his wrists, but I sent him a message anyway to let him know Rosalie was awake.

"How about this?" Enzo held up a little, yellow duck and squeezed it, so it squeaked.

I smiled, an image of my kid playing with the duck in fluffy, white bubbles and giggling flashing through my thoughts. In my mind, she had fire red hair like Rosalie and my blue eyes.

My heart clenched, and I snatched the duck from Enzo. He winked at me and moved deeper into the gift shop. I grabbed a chick magazine, a notebook with a fancy, erasable gel pen, and some fluffy slippers for Rosalie. Buying things for girls wasn't my strong suit. I was absolute shit at it because I'd never had a girl I wanted to get shit for. I consoled my worries by telling myself it was a fucking hospital gift shop. It wasn't like I could get her a Tiffany necklace.

Huh. That's not a bad idea. I made note of it as I went to the register to pay.

"Hi," the young woman behind the counter tittered, her cheeks flushing.

"Hi." I pushed my stuff toward her.

"Oh, I love ducks. This one is cute. I love the little heart on its chest."

"Yeah, it's cute," I agreed, wishing she'd hurry so I could get upstairs to Rosalie. I'd push my damn way through her door if I had to.

Enzo came up behind me with a stuffed bear in his hands.

"Cole loves duckies. He's going to use this one in the bath later."

The girl giggled as I rolled my eyes.

"It's for my girlfriend. We're having a baby soon. She's upstairs. She was in an accident and just woke up."

"Oh no!" The girl looked horrified at my words. "I hope everything works out."

"Me too," I grunted, handing her some money.

She gave me my change and put my stuff into a gift bag. Then she rang up the teddy bear Enzo handed her.

"Are you getting something for the baby too?" she asked, biting her bottom lip.

I knew she'd been checking me out, and upon hearing I had a girlfriend, she'd moved to Enzo.

He shot her a wide grin and winked. "It's for Cole's girlfriend, who is also my girlfriend. We like to share."

I shook my head at him, chuckling.

"Oh. Um…" The girl laughed and handed him his change. "Really? Like two guys and one girl."

"No, darling. There are four guys and a girl." Enzo trailed his dark eyes up her body and leaned in.

She visibly shuddered beneath his stare.

"It's fucking amazing."

Her cheeks darkened as she gaped back at him, her lips parted.

"Ever been thoroughly fucked by four men?" he continued in a low voice.

She shook her head wordlessly.

He let out a soft chuckle. "You should try it sometime." He grabbed the bear and turned his back on her, following me out the door.

"You're an asshole."

He let out a laugh and grinned. "She was all over your dick. She wanted it. I bet all you'd have to do is invite her to the bathroom across the hall, and that pussy would've been yours."

"Didn't even think about it."

We stepped into the elevator.

"But you seemed into it," I continued as the door closed.

He scoffed. "I just like fucking with people. The only girl I want is upstairs. She's it for me."

"Me too."

"Remember that time we fucked what's her name at that club?" Enzo asked.

I laughed. "Rachel Morris. I remember. She still tries to text me. She's in my third hour. I thought we were fucking gods that night. Man, I thought it wouldn't get any better than that."

"Until Rosalie."

"Until Rosalie," I agreed. "I know that shit will be fire once this shit storm passes. I have to hold onto hope."

"It'll be amazing. I'm not even worried."

"You never are," I said with a soft laugh.

"I'm Lorenzo-Fucking-De Luca."

He was. It explained it all.

CHAPTER 18

*H*er eyes were closed. Her plump lips were cracked and twisted like she was in pain.

"What's wrong with her?" I demanded as she gave a tiny whimper.

"She's still under the influence of some meds to help her with pain," Doctor Browning commented as he adjusted the cannula on her nose.

"Can you give her something else?" Mrs. Bishop asked from Rosie's other side. "She seems like she's hurting still."

Doctor Browning rattled something off to the nurse who swept out of the room. I assumed it was for more medicine, but I was too focus on my girl to pay much attention.

"Fox," Rosie croaked in the most pitiful sounding voice. Her voice cracked before she became silent.

"Baby, I'm here."

The doctor stepped aside, so I moved next to Rosalie. I gave her uninjured hand a squeeze. "I'm here. It's me. It's Fox."

She let out another soft whimper. The nurse bustled back into the room and pushed a needle into Rosalie's IV. A moment later, Rosie stopped shifting and whimpering so much and went still.

"That'll help her sleep and dull some of the pain. She has a long road ahead of her," Doctor Browning said, shaking his head. "Her vitals look good. I think she may have a rough couple of nights ahead, but she'll get through it. We'll try to provide the best comfort we can."

"And the baby?" I demanded. "Is pumping her full of all the pain meds and shit good for the baby?"

"We'll monitor everything. Rosalie will be closing out her first trimester soon, so anything can happen. Keep that in mind."

"So you're saying she could still lose the baby?" My guts churned at the information.

"Anything is possible. She's been through a lot. We can't rule it out at this point. We'll do what we can, OK?"

I nodded tightly, grateful Cole wasn't in the room. He'd lose his shit. I'd seen the cute little outfit he'd bought the baby and how desperate he was for this. If something happened to Rosalie and the baby, we might lose Cole for good.

Doctor Browning and the nurse left, leaving me with Rosalie and her parents.

"She's strong. She's going to make it," her mom murmured as she stared down at Rosalie. "She has to."

I glanced at John who sat with his head in his hands. I released Rosalie's hand and moved to sit beside him.

"How are you doing?" I asked softly, not even sure if he wanted to talk to me. I knew he was still stewing over his encounter with Cole and how he didn't want us in a relationship with Rosie. But he needed to accept, at the very least, Cole would be involved because of the baby.

"This is my fault. If I'd just let her stay. I-I overreacted that night. That punk came into my house. He ate at my table. He-He tried to take my baby girl from me," his voice cracked. "I'm not a good father. She's going to hate me when she wakes up."

"Rosalie loves you," I murmured. "Her heart is too big and sweet to ever hate you. Trust me."

John lifted his head and peered at me with his red eyes and blew out a breath. "You're a good kid, Fox. I would've loved for you and Rosalie to make something of yourselves together. Your mother and

Marcy used to sit on the patio and discuss your futures. I never thought it would be this way."

I nodded, watching Mrs. Bishop dote over Rosalie, whispering things I couldn't hear.

"You need to understand, we love Rosalie with our whole hearts. This isn't a game for us. She's it for us. I want a future with her. So do the others," I explained.

John nodded, his Adam's apple bobbing. "I'll let her decide what she wants. I won't stand in her way again."

"For what it's worth, I think you're a good dad. We all make mistakes. God knows I've made enough," I muttered.

He nodded again but remained silent. I knew the wheels in his head were spinning. I got to my feet and went back to Rosalie.

"I'm going to stay with her tonight," Mrs. Bishop said, casting me a quick, watery smile. "John and I already discussed it. He's going to go home. He hasn't been sleeping."

I nodded. "I'm going to get the guys and go. If anything changes, let me know, OK?"

"I will."

I leaned down and placed a kiss on Rosalie's forehead. "I'll see you tomorrow, baby."

I left the room quietly and made my way to Ethan's room. I knew I'd find Enzo and Cole there.

CHAPTER 19

ETHAN

"And the fourth horseman has arrived," I called out in my rough voice as Fox stepped into the room.

Enzo and Cole swiveled their heads in his direction.

Fox's hands were buried deep in his pockets, and he looked tired.

"What's going on? Is she awake?" Cole demanded.

"She's. . . not." He sounded defeated.

"What?" Enzo asked, his brows furrowed.

"What's going on?" I shifted, wincing. I still hurt, but my ass was out of here tomorrow. The moment I signed my release papers, I was heading to Rosalie's room.

"Nothing, really. She's just in a lot of pain. She's not talking. The doctor gave her some pain meds, and they put her out again." He blew out a breath and swallowed.

"She's not talking? How bad is it? The baby?" Cole's legs bounced as he waited for Fox to answer.

"The doctor said the baby isn't out of the woods yet. Their main concern is to get Rosalie comfortable and manage her pain. He said she has a long road ahead of her. She still might lose the baby." His last sentence was soft.

Cole balled his hands into fists.

My guts clenched.

"You knew it was a possibility," Enzo reminded Cole. "Keep your cool."

Cole was on his feet, his fingers in his blond hair.

"Calm down, man. They're probably just saying it as a precaution —" I started, but Cole shook his head.

"I-I can't do this shit."

"You can't go in there. She's resting—" Fox started, but Cole tugged his hair quickly.

"I-I've gotta get out of here. I've gotta go."

"Man, easy," Enzo said, finally rising to his feet. "It'll be OK."

"Fuck OK," Cole snarled. "*Nothing* is OK anymore. Can't you see that?" he asked, hysteria in his tone.

"Jesus, I knew I shouldn't have said anything," Fox murmured, shaking his head. His phone buzzed. He pulled it out and read the message, a frown on his face.

"What is it?" I asked.

"Juliet. She wants to talk to me."

"Fuck that cunt," Cole snapped, his face reddening. "I'm so sick of this shit. The moment Rosalie is well enough to leave this hospital, I'm taking her away from all this fucking shit. Her and the baby don't need to deal with this." His crazed expression landed on Enzo. "Let me just fucking do it already."

"Do what?" Fox demanded, his gaze darting between Enzo and Cole.

"We're *not* discussing this shit here." Enzo strode across the room, his expression dark. "Cole, I think you need to cool off."

"I need my girl and kid to be safe—"

"You're going to fuck this up for all of us if you don't calm the fuck down. Do you think Rosalie's parents want her jumping from one abusive prick to four guys who don't look like they have their shit together? Do you want to never see your fucking kid again? Because I bet Rosalie's parents will still have an influence on her, regardless of the shit that went down. John is the type of guy who'd push your nobody ass out into the street rather than fuck with you. Get. Your. Shit. *Together*," Enzo gritted out.

"I'm just throwing my two cents in. I love you guys and everything, but if I have to choose Rosalie or you, I'm choosing her," I called out. "I didn't almost die to get fucked over."

"No one is going to fuck you over." Enzo looked over at me. "I promise you that."

"Then Fox better shut that shit down with Juliet, and Cole better figure out his crap, because I *know* what I want." I cast an even look at my friends. "I'm *not* going to lose her again."

Cole blew out a breath and settled back into his seat. Enzo cast him an uneasy glance before returning to his. Fox moved forward and sat at the foot of my bed.

"It's just going to take time. We need to be patient," I murmured. "I love her. I love you guys. Let's take it day by day. For all of us. I don't want to lose any of you. You're my family."

"You're not going to lose us." Enzo got up and rested his forehead against mine. "I promise we'll get it sorted." He tapped my cheek lightly as was his way, and I gave his hand a feeble squeeze. He released me and moved back to his chair.

"I'm sorry. I'll get the Juliet shit worked out." Fox glared at his phone.

"Did she say she wanted to meet up and talk?" Cole grunted.

"Yeah."

"Then let's meet her. You let her suck your cock while I go look for the shit she has," Cole said. "I'll burn her fucking house down if I have to."

"That's a terrible idea," I said, shaking my head.

"It's not *that* bad," Enzo said, cocking his head.

"I am *not* letting that bitch suck my dick," Fox snapped, his face reddening. "I'm with Rosalie, and I'm certainly not going to cheat on her."

"It's not cheating." Cole looked to Enzo who nodded in agreement.

"It *is* cheating," I interjected.

"To be fair, it's getting what we need to get rid of her." Enzo rose to his feet. "I'll do it if you won't. I'll keep her occupied while you guys get the shit. Take her whole fucking computer if you have to."

"You can't be fucking serious?" I stared at the two who looked like they were actually contemplating the idea.

"Fine. Let's do it." Fox shot a message off to Juliet before I could even get out enough words to protest.

"Sorry, buddy," Cole murmured, giving me a sorrowful look. "Take care of Rosalie while we're gone."

"Sure, dickheads. I'll do just that from my hospital bed when I'm not allowed out of my fucking room. You're all fucking idiots," I called out to their backs as they turned to leave. "You're making a huge mistake. I won't cover for you. You fuck everything up, and you're on your own!"

"See you in the morning, E," Enzo said, glancing back at me as he reached the door.

Cole and Fox had already left.

"Don't do this. You have to learn. Remember what happened last time?" I whispered.

"This won't be like last time. You said you were in, remember?"

I nodded tightly.

"*This* is what *being in* looks like. We want to keep Rosalie's rep intact. You know how Juliet is. All she'll be able to do is run her mouth once we have everything. Cole *needs* this."

He was right. Cole was fit to explode. He needed to act. He had to feel like he was doing *something* worthwhile to keep Rosalie safe.

"Fine. Just... be careful."

"Where's the fun in that?"

And with those departing words, Enzo disappeared, leaving me to worry about what sort of shit they were about to get us in.

Again.

CHAPTER 20

ENZO

"She said she'll meet me at my place." Fox darkened his screen as I drove through town.

My Mercedes purred beneath us as the scenery whizzed past. I was driving way too fast but fuck it. I wanted this shit over with sooner rather than later. I'd been contemplating how to kill Juliet, and any reason at this point seemed like a good reason. The good guy inside me wanted to give her a chance. But the bad guy wanted to toy with her and pull off her wings before I lit fire to her ass.

"What's the plan?" Cole's voice was a low growl.

"She wants *me* to be there. If it's anyone else, she'll be suspicious," Fox said softly.

I caught him wincing in my rearview mirror.

"I know you don't want to do this, but it needs to be done. If we don't neutralize Juliet, she's going to show the whole school Rosalie's shit. Plus, she might spill her guts on the whole Ian situation. Not that I think she can actually get us in trouble, but it would be a shit stain on our records, especially yours, Fox. Your scholarship would probably go to hell if those videos got out."

He nodded tightly.

"You don't have to fuck her. Just keep her busy." Cole glanced over his shoulder at Fox. "Hear her out. Get as much information as you can. Try to talk some sense into her. The next step ends in splat."

"What?" Fox frowned.

I sighed and whipped the car to the side of the road. With my gaze locked on Fox's in the rearview mirror, I pulled the loaded gun out of my center console. Fox's mouth dropped open.

"I've been given a gift, Evans. *I* can take care of the problem and we'll be done with it, or you can try to smooth things over."

"Are you fucking kidding me?" Fox shouted. "You planned on *murdering* her?"

"I guess you're the determining factor in that." I quickly relayed the connection between her father and my father to Fox, who shook his head like I was insane.

"You fucking knew about this, Cole? And you're OK with it? You're going to be a *dad*, man! You think being a murderer is the best role model for a kid—"

"I'm already a murderer." Cole turned in his seat and glared at Fox. "I will kill *anyone* who gets in my way where Rosalie and my kid are concerned. Don't act all high and mighty, Fox. You're the one who wanted to torture her until she broke."

"I made a mistake. I just wanted. . ."

"You wanted her to feel as broken as you did. You blamed her. We know the story. Well, now it's time to do the shit you knew we'd have to eventually. You're in or you're out. It's that fucking simple. If you're out, get the fuck out, and we'll take care of this how it should've been taken care of from the start. If you're in, do your fucking job." I gave him an even look in the rearview mirror.

"So you think killing people is the answer?"

"Yep." Cole popped the P on the word. "We have a list. I'm not leaving this town until I've taken care of it."

"You in or out?" I asked softly. "If you're out, we're done here. Take care of Rosalie and Ethan for us. And the baby."

Cole balled his hands into fists but didn't say anything.

I turned and finally looked at Fox directly. "We're burning seconds here. In or out?"

"I fucking hate you assholes. I'm in. I meant it in the beginning, and I mean it still." He sat back in his seat, a muscle thrumming along his jaw. "But I don't want anyone fucking dying. That's some last resort shit."

"Then keep her busy. Whether she lives or dies is in your hands, Foxy." I turned around and wheeled back onto the road.

"I can't control what she does," he grumbled.

Cole let out a dark laugh. "I could if you'd let me." He was holding the gun in his hand.

"There's still time for all that," I said darkly as Fox ground his teeth in the backseat. "But let's try it this way first."

"When did you lose your damn mind, De Luca?" Fox called out.

"Who said I ever had it?"

Cole glanced over and gave me a genuine grin, which I returned. He knew exactly what I meant. Two peas in a mother fucking pod.

We dropped Fox off at his place. Then I put in a call to Emilio and let him know I was going to be stealing some shit along with breaking and entering.

"Killing her is faster," he said with a laugh. "And probably cleaner."

"I know, but I figure this might be fun."

"I thought we were trying to get rid of the drama. You think that bitch is going to be happy about being led on?"

"I certainly hope not. It's not fun if there aren't tears."

Emilio laughed again. "Kid, just kill her."

"It'll probably come to that. I just want Fox to know I tried in the beginning."

"I get it. I do. But understand your father wants to see some blood for this. You're either going to take out that bitch or you're going to take out her father. It's your choice. You know that's where it'll end up."

"I know," I murmured.

"Then have your fun. Just don't drag it out too long. Call if you need me." He clicked off, and I looked to Cole.

"Giving you shit?"

"Yep."

"Let's just kill her. I'll walk in and pop-pop. Game over."

"We'd have to be sneakier than that," I mumbled. "When it comes time to choose, it'll have to look like an accident."

"Or maybe they just fucking disappear. That's why Emilio is called The Body Snatcher, right?"

I nodded. He was. People just came up missing around him. None of the bodies were ever found. He was just that fucking good at what he did.

We pulled down the street and got out. Night had fallen, which made this shit easier. Thankfully, there weren't any cars parked in Juliet's driveway. Her parents were hardly ever home.

We'd spent time in her bedroom, so we had a decent lay of the land.

The Crofts had one security camera at their front door.

We each grabbed a knapsack from my trunk and sneaked to the back of her house through the shadows. I grabbed onto the trellis I'd climbed many times before to get into her room and heaved myself up. Cole followed. I was banking on her dumb ass leaving her window unlocked. With a gloved hand, I reached out and tried it. Sure enough, it slid open.

I went through the window with Cole behind me.

"Grab her computer," I said.

Cole grabbed her laptop and stuffed it into his bag while I riffled through her drawers, scooping up flash drives. I didn't give a shit if it was her homework or our videos. Everything was dumped into my bag.

"Keep looking for shit. I'm going to go check the study down the hall."

Cole nodded and continued searching her room. I made my way to the study and stole the laptop in there. All the other electronics and items she may have the videos on, including an iPad and another tablet were snatched as well.

When I got back to her room, Cole was stuffing a big, pink dildo into his bag.

"What the fuck are you doing with that?" I asked.

"Figured if she can't fuck herself, it might piss her off. It's the little things. Or in this case, an eight-inch silicone cock." He gave me a grin that made me chuckle.

"You're a fucking weirdo. Let's get out of here."

"Can you believe this thing has a suction cup?" he asked as we climbed off the trellis and returned to my car.

"It's almost as big as my cock."

Cole snorted. "You're not the only one with a big dick around here."

"We can sword fight about it later." I laughed.

Cole shared my mirth. "You think Fox is holding up OK?"

"Let's hope so. The last thing we need is him fucking her and her claiming he got her knocked up."

"You think she'd do that?"

"I think she'd claim he raped her. And that's worse. So we better hurry up and save his ass."

And with that, we sped off to Fox's.

CHAPTER 21

FOX

Juliet sat on my couch and peered at me with wide eyes.

"What?" I grunted from my spot on the love seat.

"Why won't you sit next to me?"

"Because I fucking hate you," I said evenly. "I thought you knew that."

Her cheeks reddened. "It doesn't have to be like this. I mean, really. What does she have that I don't?"

"How about a personality? We can start there."

Juliet rolled her eyes. "You liked fucking me, Fox. I *know* you did. You came every time." Slowly, she moved her skirt up her legs, exposing her red thong.

"I'm a guy, a warm breeze would work just as well getting me hard. Are you here to talk or be a whore?" I snapped, glaring at her.

"Both." She giggled without shame. "No one has to know what we do. Would that make it easier on you? If I became your dirty little secret?" She pushed her thong aside, showing me her shaved, pink pussy. "You let me suck your cock in the beginning when you were starting out with Rosalie."

"You sucked my dick one fucking time before Rosalie agreed to be with me, and you scraped my shit. It was literally the first day I approached Rosalie about everything. So it doesn't count."

"I wonder if she'd think the same thing." Juliet ran her finger up her slit and swirled it over her clit.

I ground my teeth. "What did you come here for, Juliet?"

"I just wanted to show you what you're missing."

"The only thing I'm missing is in a hospital bed. That ain't you, bitch."

"Such a dirty mouth. You make me so . . . wet." To prove her point, she dipped her finger into her pussy and pulled it out to show me her glistening fingertip.

"You disgust me."

"You know you'd fuck me right now if she wasn't in the picture."

"Pretty sure I wouldn't."

Come on, Enzo. Cole. Hurry the fuck up. Being stuck here with Juliet rubbing her pussy on my couch wasn't turning me on. In fact, it made me sick. All I wanted was for this shit to be over with. I wanted my life back. I wanted Rosalie home and healthy. I wanted Ethan to feel better and *be* better.

Fuck. This sucked.

Juliet got up and moved to me.

"Don't," I warned, clenching my jaw.

Where the fuck are you, Enzo?

"Are you even together with her?" She pulled her dress over her head, leaving her bare tits and pussy exposed.

I averted my eyes. "Yes."

"Is it your baby?"

"It's *our* baby," I said tightly.

"I take that as a no. Who got her knocked up? I bet it was Enzo with his giant cock and smooth talk." She straddled my lap and kissed along my neck. I pushed her away, trying to keep my shit together. I'd give them ten more minutes, and then I'd just give in and let them shoot her ass.

She remained on my lap and rubbed her tits.

"I want to come, Fox. Let me?"

"Do what you want, just not with me."

She giggled softly and rubbed her pussy with one hand and kneaded her right tit with the other.

"Tell me your cock is hard."

"It's not." That wasn't a lie. For once in my life, the fucker wasn't standing at attention.

"Let me fix it," she moaned, rubbing her pussy faster. "I want you, Fox. Fuck me, please."

"No, Juliet," I whispered, finally looking at her. "This isn't how *love* works."

"You can learn to love me," she choked out, her chest heaving as she continued to play with her snatch.

"Sweetheart." I cradled her face in my hands.

She let out a low moan.

"No one will *ever* love you."

She slowed her rubbing, her eyes glimmering with tears.

"You know why?" I growled.

"Why?" she whispered.

"Because you're the fucking devil."

I shoved her hard, and she tumbled off my lap, landing on her ass on the floor. I jumped to my feet and went to her, fisting her hair. She let out a whimper as I gripped her hair so tightly I was surprised I didn't rip some of it out. I had the intense vision of smashing her face into the floorboards until all signs of life stopped.

Maybe Cole and Enzo were onto something.

"Well, well, well. What do we have here?" Enzo called out as he leaned against the doorway to the living room. He looked like the fucking mob prince he was with his leather gloves and jacket, his black hair perfectly styled.

Cole came into the room and looked at me fisting a naked Juliet's hair and then turned to Enzo.

"Looks like the party is just getting started." Cole stepped forward and sat on the couch and slipped his phone out of his jacket pocket.

I released Juliet, and she crumpled to the floor, her hair a mess. Enzo moved deeper into the room and took a seat next to Cole.

Knowing these two were about to unleash some sort of hell, I sighed and sank onto the love seat, the three of us surrounding a naked Juliet.

"You know what would be fun?" Enzo asked, his dark-eyed gaze leveled on Juliet.

She leaned forward, eager. "What?"

"If you played with your pussy for us. Maybe we could have one last go of it before Rosalie comes home."

Juliet's eyes lit up. I shot a glare at Enzo who winked at me.

What the fuck was he up to?

"What do you want me to do?" Juliet sat up tall, all signs of her earlier tears gone, eager as fucking ever to do our bidding.

"Lie back for me. Spread your legs. Let's see that pussy." Enzo sank back against the couch cushion and gave Cole a nudge.

Cole started recording on his phone.

"What are you going to do with the video?" she asked nervously.

"Use your imagination. I'm sure you'll figure it out." Cole edged forward and trained the phone on her.

She grinned and dropped to her back, resting her weight on her elbows. I watched as her legs fell apart, her pussy on display.

"Touch yourself," Enzo commanded.

Her fingers trailed down to her pussy. She rubbed it slowly until her breathing became labored, and then she sped up, the sounds of her wet pussy around us.

I watched, disgusted, as she finger-fucked herself, her back arching off the floor with every thrust.

Enzo caught my eye and smirked at me. I had no idea what game he was playing, but Juliet was into it. He'd always been commanding with her. Hell, Enzo was commanding with everyone. It had only gotten worse lately.

Juliet tugged on a hardened nipple, her breathing rapid, her fingers moving in and out of her wet pussy, then circling her clit.

She let out a moan as she came hard, her legs falling limply to the sides. Enzo gave a slow clap as Cole stopped the recording.

"Did you like it?" she breathed out as Enzo got to his feet and towered over her.

"Not really," he answered softly.

"What?"

"You disgust me. But it was worth it."

She sat up and stared up at him.

He kneeled in front of her and brushed her hair from her face. "I have you on camera, fucking yourself. Now *I* have a little power. And I kinda like that."

Juliet swallowed and glanced at me, fear dancing in her eyes for the first time.

"What?" she repeated in a hoarse voice.

"If you try to fuck with Ethan or Rosalie—*especially* Rosalie—I *will* find you." He pulled a blade from his jacket pocket and ran it along her cheek. "I will cut your pretty, little face off, and then I will fuck your skull."

He flicked the knife across her skin. A bead of blood appeared on her cheek as she let out a gasp, her body trembling.

"Do you understand?"

"You won't beat me," she whispered. "I still have the videos."

"You mean the ones on your laptop? The ones you have on that flash drive?" Enzo pulled out a flash drive and showed it to her. "Yeah. I'm not scared of you, Juliet. But you? You should be *terrified* of me."

The bead of her blood dripped onto her thigh as she stared at Enzo, her bottom lip quivering.

"I'm going to take down Rosalie. Ian didn't finish her off, but I will. Her and that fucking abomination growing in her belly."

Cole was on his feet in a flash, his hand shooting out to smack Juliet across the face. She toppled to the floor in a heap. I jumped up in an instant, holding him back as his body shook. He jerked out of my hold and wrapped his fingers around Juliet's neck, pulling her close as she clawed at his hands, her face red.

"Fucking try me, bitch. Touch her, and your stank ass pussy on the internet will be the least of your troubles. Touch what's mine, and I will fucking end you myself."

Juliet sobbed softly on the floor as Cole released her and backed away. He sat back on the couch, his glare dark and filled with fury.

I grabbed her by the hair again as Enzo stood and idly watched.

"Get up and get out. We're done here."

She got to her feet and started to grab her clothes, but I shoved her away. She stumbled, her cheek smeared with her blood, and bounced off Enzo who did nothing to try to help her.

"No clothes for you. You can have this though." I tossed her an ugly ass crocheted blanket that could barely cover a couch cushion. My Aunt Barb had made it. It was small and wouldn't cover half Juliet's body, but it was more than the bitch deserved.

"What if something happens to me?" she asked, taking the flimsy mess of knotted yarn and tried to cover herself with it.

"Sounds like your problem. Not mine. Now get the fuck out." I glowered at her.

She glared at the three of us. "You think I'm kidding? You'll pay for this."

"Looking forward to it." Enzo gave her his signature smile. "Tell your daddy, Anthony De Luca sends his greetings. Show him your face. He'll know what it means."

Juliet hesitated for a moment before booking it out of there. I didn't know what she was worried about. It wasn't like she'd walked here. She'd have a naked drive home. I should've taken her keys too.

Enzo glanced at me. "Nice touch getting her naked."

"Fuck you. She did that shit on her own."

Enzo laughed.

"She's not done, you know," Cole said.

I nodded. I knew he was right. The bitch was digging her own grave and didn't even realize it.

"I certainly hope she fights." Enzo sank down onto the couch and grabbed the remote, flipping on the TV like nothing had happened.

"I do *so* love the torment." Cole settled back, a small, dark smile on his face that made even me shiver.

But I was in. I was still so. Fucking. In.

CHAPTER 22

ETHAN

I groaned as my feet touched the cold hospital room floor.

"Ethan, you need to put these socks on," Nurse Annoying called out to me.

"Fuck the socks. I can't even wipe my own ass," I shot back at her. "How the hell am I going to put on socks?"

She let out a huff and kneeled in front of me. I let her put the ugly, yellow, gripper socks on me.

"I'm going home," I said. "Not dancing at the fucking nursing home. My feet aren't going to fit into my shoes with these thick ass things on."

She closed her eyes for a moment to summon more patience. I knew I was giving her shit. But fuck, the woman annoyed me. I was pretty sure she took great pleasure pulling the catheter out of my cock once the doc gave her permission.

"I'll take it from here," Enzo said, coming into the room.

Nurse Annoying got to her feet and left the room after shaking her head at me.

"You giving the staff shit?" Enzo asked as I stood up with a wince. He bent in front of me and held my gray sweats out so I could step into them.

"I don't mean to. Coming down from the narcotics has me a bit fucked right now. Can you believe I'm only being sent home with some non-narcotic shit? How the hell am I going to last on ibuprofen?"

"You'll be fine. I've got some choice weed." Enzo pulled my pants up for me and moved behind me to undo my hospital gown.

"Better than nothing," I grunted.

I hated I was an addict. Like, I fucking loathed it. But getting your ass pounded as a kid, losing your virginity before you could read, and then murdering your old man tended to leave deeper than flesh scars. I was living proof of that. I'd spent the better part of my life self-medicating. And when I wasn't, my worthless parents were shooting me up. Even as a kid, I was wasted. It made it easier for their friends to fuck me.

Who was I kidding though? I was born an addict. The system failed me from the start. They knew my mother was a worthless junkie and left me with her. My problems started before I'd drawn in my first fucking breath.

My mind went to a dark place as memories of being hurt as a kid flooded my thoughts.

"Look at him fight," one of the men in the room laughed.

"Boy sure does have a lot of fight in him. Let's tie him up. See how he fights then. . ."

Obviously, there were times when they liked the struggle. It didn't matter. I always fought like hell too. Nightmares. It was the shit nightmares were made of. Needless to say, I had issues. A lot of fucking issues. But when I met Rosalie, it changed. She soothed my broken soul. She mended the pieces, putting me back together.

Almost losing her had broken me all over again. I was hoping the fix this time would be permanent. I just needed to get over this awful fucking roadblock. *The addiction.*

For her, I'd do it. I'd get help sooner rather than later, so I could hold her at night. She was going to need me, and I couldn't fail her. Not again. *God, not again.*

"Here." Enzo dragged my black t-shirt over my head.

I sat down and let him put my shoes on my feet.

"You *almost* look good, Masters."

I chuckled. "Where are Fox and Cole?"

"Waiting for Rosalie's parents to leave her room. They're in the lounge. I told them I'd come get you."

I nodded. I'd agreed to go to Enzo's. My parents were moving my belongings there at that very moment.

"Are you the one who paid my hospital bill?" I asked, studying Enzo.

"Why would you think that?"

"Man, did you? I owe you a shit ton—"

"Listen. You paid your debt in blood and tears. We're family. You saved our girl. You owe me *nothing*, Ethan. Ever. You got it?"

I nodded, my throat tight.

"Don't you fucking cry on me."

I reached out for him, and he came at me, arms open.

"Thank you. My parents wouldn't have been able to afford—"

"I got you, man. Always. We're even. Don't ever bring it up again, OK?" He gave me a gentle hug before pulling away.

I nodded. "I signed my release papers. I'm ready to go."

Enzo strolled across the room and grabbed my phone off the bedside table and stuffed it into my pocket. My parents had already taken everything but my jacket and change of clothes.

"Ready?" he asked.

"Yes," I breathed out, eager to finally get to see Rosalie.

"THEY'RE GONE," Fox called out as we sat in the waiting room. "We can go in."

Cole was the first one to his feet and out the door.

"Guess he's not eager or anything," Fox grumbled, following him.

He stopped next to me and helped me stand. I offered him a sheepish smile.

"Sorry. I'm hoping this helpless shit doesn't last long."

"It could last a decade, man. As long as you're here with us." He gave me an earnest look as he helped me walk in front of him. I'd refused the wheelchair.

My body was still stiff and aching, but I was as eager to see Rosalie as everyone else was. I was just slower getting there.

Enzo and Fox didn't push me and kept at my pace. I was surprised to see Cole standing outside her room, a frown on his face.

"I thought you'd already be in there," I said as we stopped beside him.

"I-I can't."

"What?" Fox looked at him then at us before looking back at him. "Why?"

"Because I'm the supreme fuck up. I thought I was ready for this moment, but what if she tells me to kick rocks? What will I do?"

"She's not going to tell you that," I said. "She loves you. I would know."

"How?" He peered over at me, worry on his face.

"When I was making love to her, she called out your name." It was a joke I hoped would lighten his mood.

He cracked a small smile at me as the other guys chuckled.

"She did not."

"Ask her yourself," I said, nodding to the door.

He licked his lips for a moment before he hauled in a deep breath, pushed the door open, and stepped into the room. We followed him in. I wasn't sure what I expected to see, but Rosalie in a hospital bed, her face bruised and about a million wires coming off her wasn't it. Her body was so small and still in the metal frame.

Enzo gripped my elbow as I faltered.

"Hey, Rosie," Fox called out as she cracked her pretty, green eyes open.

Confusion and pain flashed in their jade depths. Then they flickered closed once more.

And my heart shuttered along with them.

Everything would change. Everything *had* changed. I didn't know what was going to happen, just that whatever it was, I would be there.

Nothing would stop me.

At least that's what I told myself as I stood staring down at the girl who owned my heart, that familiar ache for a chemical escape gnawing at my soul.

To Be Continued in In Chaos. Out Now!

Please consider leaving your review!

IN CHAOS

A BLACK FALLS HIGH NOVEL

Some things are better left unsaid. Others demand chaos. Good thing I excel at both.

Everything fell apart before we were able to pull ourselves together.

When tragedy demands my silence, I have no choice but to give it because losing a life also means saving so many more.

I finally have everything I want. Having my best friend back is a dream come true. But everything at Black Falls High comes at a price, and these boys are mine. I'd do anything for them.

Even in ruins. In silence. I'll bring the chaos.

In Chaos is a dark bully romance with four guys and one girl. Due to dark subject matter, reader discretion is advised.

Get In Chaos here:
Books2read.com/inchaos

ACKNOWLEDGMENTS

Thank you to my readers. Yes! You! You made this possible.

Thanks to my alpha readers. You guys keep all my crazy from spilling onto the pages. Without you guys, there would be more pitchforks and fires in my life.

To my editor, I apologize for being painfully unorganized. You make my words shine though, so thank you.

And finally, a thank you to my family. Thank you for tiptoeing past my office without interrupting my brain vomit. To my husband, thanks for your support and cute attempts to help me. I'm not using your weird ideas, but they're a nice distraction.

ABOUT THE AUTHOR

Affectionately dubbed Queen of Cliffy, Suspense, Heartbreak, and Torture by her readers, USA Today bestselling author K.G. Reuss is known mostly for making readers ugly cry with her writing. A cemetery creeper and ghost enthusiast, K.G. spends most of her time toeing the line between imagination and forced adulthood.

After a stint in college in Iowa, K.G. moved back to her home in Michigan to work in emergency medicine. She's currently raising three small ghouls and is married to a vampire overlord (not really but maybe he could be someday).

K.G. is the author of Black Falls High, Kings of Bolten, The Boys of Chapel Crest, The Everlasting Chronicles series, Emissary of the Devil series, The Chronicles of Winterset series, Barely Breathing with a ridiculous amount of other series set to be released.

Join me in my Facebook reader group here:

https://www.facebook.com/groups/streetteamkgreuss
Sign up for my newsletter here:
https://tinyletter.com/authorkgreuss
Follow me on TikTok:
https://vm.tiktok.com/ZMeY8asPc

ALSO BY K.G. REUSS

Emissary of the Devil: Testimony of the Damned

Emissary of the Devil: Testimony of the Blessed

Emissary of the Devil: Gospel of the Fallen

The Everlasting Chronicles: Dead Silence

The Everlasting Chronicles: Shadow Song

The Everlasting Chronicles: Grave Secrets

The Everlasting Chronicles: Soul Bound

The Chronicles of Winterset: Oracle

The Chronicles of Winterset: Tempest

Black Falls High: In Ruins

Black Falls High: In Silence

Black Falls High: In Pieces

Black Falls High: In Chaos

Hard Pass

Kings of Bolten: Dirty Little Secrets

Barely Breathing

The Middle Road

Seven Minutes in Heaven

www.ingramcontent.com/pod-product-compliance
Lightning Source LLC
Chambersburg PA
CBHW031541310726
48971CB00008B/2579